This is a work of fiction. S
events are entirely coincid

THE UNTOLD STOR
CHARLES

First edition. December 8, 2023.

Copyright © 2023 Jagdish Krishanlal Arora.

ISBN: 979-8223766544

Written by Jagdish Krishanlal Arora.

Also by Jagdish Krishanlal Arora

Basic Inorganic and Organic Chemistry
Book of Jokes
Car Insurance and Claims
Digital Electronics, Computer Architecture and Microprocessor Design Principles
Guided Meditation and Yoga
The Bible and Jesus Christ
Unity Quest
From Oasis to Global Stage: The Evolution of Arab Civilization
Secrets of Mount Kailash, Bermuda Triangle and the Lost City of Atlantis
Visitors from Outer Space
Motivation
The Aliens and God Theory
The Lunar Voyager
Queen Elizabeth II and the British Monarchy
Vegetable Gardening, Salads and Recipes
How to End The War in Ukraine
The Old and New World Order
Galactic Odyssey
Travelling to Mars in the Cosmic Odyssey 2050
Romance Pays Off

How the Universe Works
Mental Health and Well Being
Ancient History of Mars
The Nexus
Basic and Advanced Physics
Administrative Law
Calculus
A Watery Mystery
Romantic Conflicts
Thieves of Palestine
Love in Chicago
WordPress Design and Development
Travellers Guide to Mount Kailash
Become a Better Writer With Creative Writing
Emerging Trends in Carbon Emission Reduction
India Independence Through Non Violence
Copyright, Patents, Trademarks and Trade Secret Laws
The Untold Story of Diana and Prince Charles

Table of Contents

The Untold Story of Diana and Prince Charles 1
Introduction 3
Chapter 1: A Royal Arrival - Prince Charles's Birth......... 11
Chapter 2: The Coronation...14
Chapter 3: The Royal Tour...16
Chapter 4: A Longtime Connection...................................18
Chapter 5: Decades of Duty: Queen Elizabeth's Reign from 1956 to 1972..21
Chapter 6: Uncharted Paths...24
Chapter 7: Althorp Encounter 30
Chapter 8: Ski Weekend Secrets...33
Chapter 9: Mutual Friend's Estate......................................37
Chapter 10: Balmoral Revelation 40
Chapter 11: Windsor Castle Proposal 43
Chapter 12: Royal Wedding..47
Chapter 13: Birth of Prince William 52
Chapter 14: Birth of Prince Harry......................................55
Chapter 15: Marital Troubles 60
Chapter 16: Tell-All Revelation 65
Chapter 17: The Glums in South Korea............................72
Chapter 18: Separation Announcement 75
Chapter 19: Financial Settlement 78
Chapter 20: Liberated Post-Royal Life 81
Chapter 21: The Tragic End of a Princess-Diana's Tragic End to a Royal Journey 84
Chapter 22: The Unfinished Tale.......................................88
Chapter 23: A New Chapter Begins...................................90

THE UNTOLD STORY OF DIANA AND PRINCE CHARLES

In Loving Memory of Princess Diana

BY

JAGDISH KRISHANLAL ARORA

techbagg@outlook.com

Princess Diana

Introduction

In the grand tapestry of British royalty, one chapter emerges as a captivating narrative of love, turmoil, and enduring legacy. The story begins at Althorp House in November 1977, were Prince Charles encounters Lady Diana, unknowingly setting the stage for a tumultuous romance. Ski Weekend Secrets in February 1978 reveal the complexities of royal relationships, as Charles's connection with Diana deepens despite the end of his previous relationship.

The stage shifts to July 1980 at Philip de Pass's estate, where a pivotal conversation about Lord Mountbatten's death propels Charles and Diana's relationship into the public eye at Balmoral in September 1980. The fairy tale facade of their union is further tested with Charles's proposal at Windsor Castle in February 1981, drawing global attention and questioning the authenticity of their love.

As the royal wedding unfolds at Westminster Abbey in July 1981, doubts linger in Diana's mind, foreshadowing the challenges ahead. Joy turns to struggle with the birth of Prince William in June 1982, marking the onset of Diana's postpartum depression. Prince Harry's arrival in September 1984 amplifies the strains on their marriage, leading to extramarital affairs in 1986.

Tell-All Revelation in May 1992 exposes the collapse of Charles and Diana's marriage, setting the stage for an official separation announced by Prime Minister John Major in

December 1992. Financial Settlement in August 1996 finalizes their divorce, liberating Diana into a post-royal life cut short tragically in August 1997.

Camilla Rosemary Shand, now widely known as Camilla Parker Bowles, emerged onto the stage of British aristocracy with a background as diverse as the realms in which she would later play a significant role. Born on July 17, 1947, in King's College Hospital, London, she was the eldest child of Major Bruce Shand and his wife, Rosalind Cubitt. Camilla spent her formative years in East Sussex, at the family's country home, The Laines, and later in South Kensington, where the Shand family resided.

Education played a pivotal role in shaping Camilla's early years. She attended Dumbrells School, a co-educational boarding school in Surrey, where she cultivated a passion for equestrian activities. The influence of her family's equestrian background, coupled with her own interest, would later become a prominent facet of Camilla's life.

Camilla's educational journey extended beyond British borders. She ventured to Switzerland, where she attended the Mon Fertile finishing school in Tolochenaz, developing a cosmopolitan outlook that would serve her well in the circles she would come to navigate. Subsequently, she continued her education in France, rounding out a curriculum that reflected the refined pursuits of an English debutante.

In the early 1970s, Camilla's life took a significant turn when she crossed paths with British Army officer Andrew Parker Bowles. Their courtship culminated in marriage in 1973, and Camilla became the wife of a military man deeply entrenched in the traditions of British service. The union introduced her to the intricacies of military life, with Andrew's career demanding periodic separations due to deployments.

Despite the façade of marital stability, the union faced its own set of challenges. Both Camilla and Andrew engaged in extramarital affairs, setting the stage for a narrative that would later intertwine with the future King of England, Prince Charles.

Conversations within the Parker Bowles marriage mirrored the complexities of relationships subjected to the pressures of societal expectations and personal desires. The strains on their marriage led to a formal separation in 1994 and eventual divorce in 1995. Camilla, now free from the constraints of her first marriage, found herself in a position that would thrust her into the public eye and the scrutinizing gaze of the British public.

The romantic entanglement between Camilla and Prince Charles had woven its threads through the years, transcending the bounds of each of their respective marriages. Conversations, often discreet and hidden from the public, unfolded against a backdrop of duty, tradition, and the tumultuous nature of royal relationships.

The years preceding Camilla's divorce marked a period of uncharted territory. The spotlight, once avoided, now beckoned her into a new role one that carried both admiration and controversy. Conversations within royal circles speculated on the evolving dynamics of the Prince's personal life, hinting at a future that would see Camilla play a more visible part in the narrative of the British monarchy.

As the 1990s unfolded, Camilla Parker Bowles became a figurehead in the royal soap opera, her life scrutinized, her every move analysed by the public and the media. Conversations within the press shifted from discreet whispers to bold headlines, as the complexities of royal relationships unfolded in the public eye.

The saga of Camilla Parker Bowles, marked by her upbringing in the English countryside, her cosmopolitan education, a marriage shrouded in extramarital affairs, and a romantic liaison with the heir to the throne, highlighted the intricate interplay of personal choices and public expectations. Camilla's journey from the shadows to the spotlight would continue to unfold, leaving an indelible mark on the narrative of the British monarchy.

Parallelly, Prince Charles's enduring connection with Camilla unfolds from their early encounters in 1971 to their official union in 2005. The narrative concludes with the tragic end of Princess Diana on August 31, 1997, becoming a pivotal moment for Queen Elizabeth. The chapter reflects on the monarchy's resilience, adapting to the complexities of personal relationships and public scrutiny.

In the end it captures the essence of love's triumphs and trials, the monarchy's endurance in times of turmoil, and the indelible legacy left by Princess Diana. The royal narrative weaves a tapestry of human emotions within the grandeur of palace walls, marking a significant chapter in the annals of British history.

The idyllic surroundings of Park House Hotel in Sandringham, Norfolk, England, bore witness to the entrance of a figure who would captivate the world's imagination. Diana Frances Spencer, born on July 1, 1961, heralded the beginning of a life that would navigate the corridors of royalty, marked by both triumphs and tribulations.

Diana's arrival into the world was nestled within the aristocratic lineage of the Spencer family. Her father, the Earl Spencer, provided the familial backdrop against which her early years unfolded. The sprawling estate of Althorp House, with its rich history and picturesque landscapes, became the canvas upon which the tapestry of Diana's childhood was woven.

In the embrace of this aristocratic haven, Diana's early life was characterized by the privileges that accompanied her noble birth. Park House, a part of the Sandringham Estate, served as the stage for her formative years. The idyllic Norfolk countryside provided a backdrop for a childhood steeped in tradition, where echoes of generations past resonated through the stately halls.

However, Diana's life took a turn with the dissolution of her parents' marriage when she was just seven years old. The separation cast a shadow over the grandeur of her surroundings, introducing an element of familial discord that would later shape her understanding of love and commitment.

Education, a cornerstone of aristocratic upbringing, beckoned Diana as she entered her adolescent years. Riddlesworth Hall School, an all-girls boarding school in Norfolk, became the initial crucible of her education. The institutional rigors were balanced by the rural charm of the English countryside, laying the foundation for the young Spencer's journey into adulthood.

Diana's educational pursuits continued at West Heath School, a progressive institution that fostered independent thinking. However, her academic journey was cut short, and at the age of 16, she took her leave from formal education. This juncture marked the beginning of a more unscripted chapter in Diana's life, one that would see her stepping onto the bustling stage of London when she turned 18.

The transition to London was a pivotal moment in Diana's journey. The bustling metropolis, with its cosmopolitan allure, offered a departure from the tranquillity of her aristocratic upbringing. The move represented a step into the broader world, one beyond the manicured lawns of Althorp House and the protective cocoon of Norfolk.

Conversations within aristocratic circles and the broader societal context buzzed with speculation about the young Diana Spencer. Her arrival in London, a city steeped in history and pulsating with modernity, set the stage for a narrative that would soon intersect with the destiny of the royal family.

As Diana embraced the challenges and opportunities that London presented, little did she know that her life's journey was hurtling toward a collision with the heart of royalty. The echoes of her early life, from the grandeur of Park House to the educational halls of West Heath, served as the prologue to a tale that would unfold on the grandest stage of them all the British monarchy.

Diana, Princess of Wales, left an indelible mark on the royal family, introducing a compassionate and rebellious spirit that defied traditional norms. This transformative chapter unfolded against the backdrop of specific dates, marking key moments in Diana's journey as a humanitarian and a catalyst for change.

1987: Diana's Compassionate Touch

In 1987, during the early years of the AIDS epidemic, Princess Diana made a groundbreaking move that would challenge perceptions and ignite conversations. Her visit to an AIDS hospice in London marked a pivotal moment as she fearlessly interacted with patients, touching and hugging them. This compassionate gesture, captured in photographs, became a symbol of Diana's commitment to destigmatizing AIDS and promoting understanding.

1991: The Campaign for Change

Princess Diana continued to champion the cause of AIDS awareness. In 1991, she opened the Landmark AIDS Centre at Mildmay Hospital, underscoring her dedication to supporting institutions focused on combating the disease. These events showcased her rebellion against the reluctance to address AIDS openly within the royal family and society at large.

1997: Landmines and Legacy

In 1997, Diana took on another challenging cause landmines. Her involvement in the campaign to ban landmines brought international attention to the devastating impact of these weapons. The global conversation around the Ottawa Treaty, seeking to outlaw anti-personnel landmines, gained momentum with Diana's influential support.

1998: Robin Cook's Tribute

On January 27, 1998, in the House of Commons, Robin Cook, the Foreign Secretary, paid tribute to Princess Diana's significant contribution to the campaign against landmines. His acknowledgment underscored Diana's ability to leverage her royal status to effect legislative change, transcending the traditional boundaries of the monarchy.

1998: The Ottawa Treaty

On March 1, 1998, the UK ratified the Ottawa Treaty to ban anti-personnel landmines. Diana's advocacy played a crucial role in garnering public and political support for this landmark treaty. Her commitment to causes that went beyond conventional royal concerns marked a legacy that extended far beyond ceremonial duties.

Princess Diana's rebellion against royal conventions and her commitment to humanitarian causes were punctuated by these key dates. Each event became a milestone in her journey a journey that demonstrated the transformative power of compassion and empathy within the realm of royalty.

Chapter 1: A Royal Arrival - Prince Charles's Birth

November 14, 1948

Amidst the post-war jubilation and the winds of change sweeping through the British monarchy, a significant event unfolded at Buckingham Palace the birth of Prince Charles Philip Arthur George. Born on November 14, 1948, Prince Charles marked the beginning of a new chapter in the royal lineage.

Conversations within the palace walls buzzed with anticipation and excitement. The birth of the heir apparent was not merely a family affair; it held profound implications for the continuity and stability of the monarchy. As the news of Princess Elizabeth's labor spread, dignitaries, courtiers, and commoners alike awaited the announcement that would resonate far beyond the confines of Buckingham Palace.

In the early hours of the morning, on November 14, Princess Elizabeth, then 22 years old, went into labor. Prince Philip, the Duke of Edinburgh, anxiously paced the corridors, awaiting news of the birth. The scene was set for a royal drama that would capture the hearts of the nation.

At 9:14 PM, the cry of a newborn prince echoed through the halls of Buckingham Palace. The birth was officially announced through a proclamation placed on the palace railings. The formal notice, signed by the attending physicians, heralded the arrival of the first child of Princess Elizabeth and

Prince Philip. The proclamation, steeped in tradition, was the precursor to the modern practice of announcing royal births via easel outside Buckingham Palace.

Conversations among the British public reflected a mix of excitement and curiosity. The birth of a royal heir was an event of national significance, bringing a sense of continuity and tradition at a time when the world was undergoing rapid changes. Newspapers carried headlines that celebrated the birth, and radio broadcasts conveyed the news to the far reaches of the Commonwealth.

The young prince's name, Charles Philip Arthur George, was carefully chosen to honour his grandfather, Prince Andrew of Greece and Denmark, and his father, Prince Philip. The name "Charles" carried centuries of royal history, invoking the spirits of past kings and princes. Prince Charles's birth not only added a new member to the royal family but also bestowed upon him the weight of legacy and expectation.

In the days that followed, Buckingham Palace became a focal point of celebration. Well-wishers, citizens, and foreign dignitaries sent their regards, marking the birth as a moment of shared joy. The bells of Westminster Abbey rang in honour of the prince, and gun salutes reverberated across London.

Conversations within the royal family centred on the responsibilities that lay ahead for young Prince Charles. As the firstborn, his upbringing and education would be closely scrutinized, with an eye toward preparing him for the eventual role he would inherit.

Prince Charles's birth symbolized hope, continuity, and a connection to the past. The public's fascination with the royal family deepened, and the infant prince became a symbol of the

THE UNTOLD STORY OF DIANA AND PRINCE CHARLES

monarchy's enduring relevance. The birth of Prince Charles, on that November day in 1948, set in motion a journey that would eventually lead him to the apex of the British monarchy.

Chapter 2: The Coronation

June 2, 1953

The sun-drenched morning of June 2, 1953, dawned upon Westminster Abbey, where the grandeur of tradition and the weight of history converged for a defining moment the coronation of Queen Elizabeth II. The air buzzed with anticipation as dignitaries, aristocrats, and commoners gathered to witness the ascension of a young queen to the throne.

Amidst the opulent setting, Queen Elizabeth II's regal aura was palpable. Dressed in a shimmering gown, the St. Edward's Crown rested solemnly on her head, symbolizing not only a personal achievement but also a beacon of hope for a nation recovering from the scars of World War II. The ceremony was not merely a spectacle; it was a testament to the resilience of a nation and the dawn of a new era.

The conversations that echoed within the hallowed halls went beyond the ceremonial protocols. Advisers huddled, discussing the intricacies of navigating post-war Britain. The Queen, at the helm of this historical juncture, engaged in thoughtful dialogue with her trusted confidantes. The burden of leading a nation, rebuilding itself physically and emotionally, was a shared concern that threaded through these conversations.

As the Archbishop of Canterbury anointed the Queen with holy oil, the words uttered carried not just the weight of religious tradition but also the hopes of a people yearning for stability. The orb and sceptre handed to her symbolized not only sovereign power but also the delicate equilibrium between preserving age-old customs and adapting to the demands of a changing world.

In the midst of this monumental event, the Queen's conversations with her advisers reflected a keen awareness of the challenges ahead. The post-war landscape called for a monarch who could embody tradition while steering the nation towards progress. Discussions touched upon the delicate balance required to uphold the monarchy's historical significance while embracing the winds of change.

The robed figures, the soaring choir, and the ancient walls of Westminster Abbey bore witness to a moment frozen in time. The Queen's words, exchanged in quiet conversations, were laden with the understanding that her reign was not just a continuation but a redefinition of the monarchy's role in the modern era.

The Coronation Chapter encapsulates not only the splendour of the event but also the nuanced conversations that unfolded behind the scenes. June 2, 1953, marked the beginning of a reign characterized by resilience, adaptability, and a profound sense of duty a chapter in the grand narrative of Queen Elizabeth II's enduring legacy.

Chapter 3: The Royal Tour

1954-1955 As the pages turned in the early chapters of Queen Elizabeth II's reign, a defining narrative unfolded the Royal Tour of the Commonwealth. Spanning from 1954 to 1955, this period was marked by diplomatic intricacies, strategic conversations, and the evolving role of the monarchy in a world emerging from the shadows of war.

The journey began as Queen Elizabeth set foot on Australian soil in 1954, a momentous occasion that transcended mere ceremonial duties. Conversations behind the scenes delved into the diplomatic strategies employed to strengthen ties with Commonwealth nations. The Queen, in dialogue with her advisors, recognized the transformative power of these visits, envisioning a monarchy that went beyond symbolic representation.

Dates etched in history, such as the Queen's visit to Australia in 1954 and New Zealand in 1955, became not just chronological markers but pivotal moments in the ongoing discourse about the modernization of the Crown. The Royal Tour was more than a display of regal splendour it was a carefully choreographed dance of diplomacy, a testament to the Queen's commitment to unity in a world rife with geopolitical challenges.

Conversations within the royal entourage touched upon the nuances of cultural diplomacy, acknowledging the diversity within the Commonwealth. The Queen's interactions with dignitaries, commoners, and leaders shaped the narrative of a monarchy adapting to the realities of a changing world. The dialogue extended beyond palace walls, resonating with the public's perception of a monarch who was not only a custodian of tradition but also a bridge to a future where the Crown played a relevant and unifying role.

The Royal Tour Chapter reflects a monarch cognizant of the power of her presence on the global stage. The Queen's conversations were not confined to formal ceremonies; they embraced the pulse of the nations she visited. Each handshake, each exchange, wove a narrative of a Queen who understood the evolving dynamics of the Commonwealth and the need for the monarchy to resonate with the aspirations of its people.

This chapter encapsulates the essence of those transformative years a journey that not only spanned continents but also transcended the traditional boundaries of monarchy, setting the stage for a reign defined by adaptability, unity, and a keen sense of diplomatic prowess.

Chapter 4: A Longtime Connection

1971 - 1973

The hallowed halls of London's elite social circles echoed with the laughter and chatter of the early 1970s. Among the glittering array of young aristocrats and debutantes, two figures stood out Prince Charles and Camilla Shand. Little did the world know that within these circles, a connection was quietly forming, a connection that would weave its way through the tapestry of time.

It was 1971 when Prince Charles first encountered Camilla, known to her peers as Camilla Shand. Their introduction, orchestrated by the intricacies of aristocratic social events, marked the beginning of a friendship that transcended the boundaries of conventional royalty. The young Prince, with his earnest demeanour and a touch of shyness, found a kindred spirit in Camilla, whose wit and charm were as enchanting as the moonlit dances they shared.

As they navigated the swirl of social events, Charles and Camilla discovered shared interests that became the cornerstone of their burgeoning connection. Conversations, often sparked by a shared passion for the arts and a love for outdoor pursuits, unfolded against the backdrop of opulent ballrooms and stately gardens. The laughter that echoed through these conversations would become the melody of a friendship that defied the constraints of royalty.

Amid the grandeur of royal responsibilities, Charles found solace in Camilla's company. Their friendship deepened, becoming a source of support and companionship during pivotal moments in Charles's early life. The heir to the throne, burdened by the weight of expectations, discovered in Camilla a confidante who understood the nuances of his journey.

One evening, beneath the glittering chandeliers of a grand reception, Charles and Camilla engaged in a conversation that would resonate through the corridors of time. "Camilla, your company is a respite from the formality of palace life. In your laughter, I find a genuine connection that transcends the duties that come with my title," Charles remarked, his words carrying a sincerity that laid bare the depth of their bond.

Camilla, with a twinkle in her eye, replied, "Charles, life within these circles can be stifling. In our conversations, I discover a kindred spirit who sees beyond the trappings of royalty. Our laughter is a rebellion against the constraints that seek to define us."

Their connection, though budding, faced the inevitable challenges of a world governed by tradition and expectations. Charles, ever aware of his royal duties, and Camilla, navigating the complexities of societal norms, found solace in stolen moments of laughter and shared glances that spoke volumes.

The years 1971 to 1973 saw the roots of a relationship that would endure the test of time. Charles and Camilla's connection, forged in the fires of aristocratic social circles, became a defining aspect of Charles's personal narrative. Little did they know that these early conversations, marked by shared interests and genuine camaraderie, would lay the foundation for a relationship that would weather the storms of royal scrutiny and societal expectations.

Chapter 5: Decades of Duty: Queen Elizabeth's Reign from 1956 to 1972

The years spanning from 1956 to 1972 marked a pivotal era in Queen Elizabeth II's reign a period of dynamic change, cultural shifts, and challenges that tested the resilience of the monarchy. This chapter unravels the Queen's steadfast dedication to her role, navigating an evolving world with exact dates and significant events.

1956: The Suez Crisis and Royal Diplomacy

In 1956, Queen Elizabeth found herself at the epicentre of diplomatic turbulence during the Suez Crisis. Conversations within the palace walls centred on the delicate balance between political neutrality and the Crown's role in international affairs. The Queen's measured responses and behind-the-scenes consultations showcased her evolving role as a symbol of stability.

1957: The Commonwealth Tours

Queen Elizabeth's commitment to the Commonwealth took centre stage in 1957 with extensive tours, reinforcing bonds with member nations. From Ghana to Canada, the Queen's conversations during these visits reflected the changing dynamics within the Commonwealth, setting the tone for a collaborative and interconnected monarchy.

1960: The New Decade Unfolds

As the 1960s dawned, the monarchy faced a shifting cultural landscape. Conversations about modernization and the royal family's public image gained prominence. The Queen, cognizant of these discussions, embraced televised Christmas broadcasts, inviting the public into the private realm of the royal family.

1969: Prince Charles's Investiture

A defining moment occurred in 1969 with the investiture of Prince Charles as the Prince of Wales. The ceremony in Caernarfon Castle, Wales, showcased the delicate balance between tradition and the aspirations of a new generation. Conversations surrounding the investiture addressed the evolving role of the heir apparent.

1972: The UK Joins the European Communities

In 1972, conversations within the royal circles and the wider public sphere focused on the United Kingdom's accession to the European Communities. The Queen's role in this constitutional milestone underscored the monarchy's connection to national decisions, prompting discussions about the evolving nature of British identity.

Navigating Family and Duty

Amidst these geopolitical events, Queen Elizabeth navigated the complexities of family life. The birth of Prince Andrew in 1960 and Prince Edward in 1964 added joyous chapters to the royal narrative. Conversations within the royal family echoed the Queen's dedication to balancing maternal duties with her role as a constitutional monarch.

Adapting to Cultural Shifts

Conversations about the monarchy's relevance echoed in the face of cultural shifts, including the rise of youth culture and societal changes. The Queen's ability to adapt to these shifts, symbolized by her attendance at cultural events and engagements with contemporary figures, showcased a monarchy in tune with the times.

In these tumultuous and transformative years, Queen Elizabeth II emerged as a symbol of continuity, adaptability, and duty. Conversations within the royal household and on the global stage reflected a monarch navigating the complexities of a changing world, laying the groundwork for a reign that would span decades with grace and resilience.

Chapter 6: Uncharted Paths

1973 – 1974

HMS Bronington Commissioning:

Date: February 15, 1974

Event: HMS Bronington, a minesweeper, was commissioned into the Royal Navy. Prince Charles served on board as a Lieutenant during this time.

Prince Charles's First Command:

Date: June 14, 1976

Event: Prince Charles took command of the coastal minehunter HMS Bronington for six months as part of his naval career.

HMS Jupiter Sea Trials:

Date: January 20, 1975

Event: The Royal Navy's destroyer, HMS Jupiter, underwent sea trials in early 1975. It was a part of routine testing and readiness exercises.

Exercise Purple Warrior:

Date: September 5, 1973

Event: The Royal Navy conducted Exercise Purple Warrior, a large-scale naval exercise involving various vessels. It aimed to enhance the Navy's operational capabilities.

HMS Norfolk's Antarctic Patrol:

Date: December 2, 1974

Event: HMS Norfolk, a County-class guided-missile destroyer, patrolled the Antarctic waters. This deployment was part of the Royal Navy's global presence and surveillance efforts.

HMS Hermes Caribbean Deployment:

Date: August 17, 1973

Event: HMS Hermes, a Royal Navy aircraft carrier, was deployed to the Caribbean for training exercises and to demonstrate the UK's commitment to the region.

The corridors of royal duty echoed with a sense of change as the early 1970s unfolded. Prince Charles, heir to the throne, embarked on a naval career a path laden with responsibilities and expectations. Simultaneously, Camilla, now Camilla Parker Bowles, found herself stepping into the realms of matrimony with Andrew Parker Bowles in 1973. As the wheels of fate turned, the paths of Charles and Camilla seemed to diverge, setting the stage for a chapter marked by uncharted territories.

In the wake of Charles's naval pursuits, conversations between the prince and Camilla underwent a subtle transformation. The exuberance of their youth, once manifested in carefree laughter and shared adventures, now carried a subtle undercurrent of longing. As Charles navigated the vast expanse of the sea, duty-bound and tethered to the expectations of royalty, his thoughts often wandered to the connection that seemed to transcend the boundaries of convention.

Letters, carefully composed with ink on parchment, became the vessels that carried the unspoken sentiments between Charles and Camilla. In the quiet solitude of naval ships and the grandeur of royal palaces, their words bridged the physical distance that now separated them. Conversations, once animated by shared moments, now unfolded through the written word a testament to the enduring bond that defied the constraints of time and duty.

One such letter, written by Charles during a particularly arduous naval assignment, encapsulated the essence of their uncharted paths. "Camilla, as the waves carry me away, my thoughts find their anchor in the memories of our laughter. The path I tread may be dictated by duty, but the yearning for a connection beyond these obligations remains ever-present," he penned, the ink capturing the nuances of a prince torn between duty and desire.

Camilla, in her replies, offered words of understanding and encouragement. "Charles, our paths may seem to diverge, but the threads of our connection remain unbroken. Marriage has brought its own challenges, yet the flame of our camaraderie refuses to be extinguished. Let the winds of change guide us, for our destinies are intertwined," she wrote, the sentiments woven into each carefully chosen phrase.

The year 1974 brought forth events that further shaped the uncharted paths of Charles and Camilla. Conversations about duty, love, and the complexities of navigating societal expectations echoed through their exchanges. The world, largely unaware of the intricacies of these written dialogues, continued to observe the unfolding narratives of royal lives.

As the pages of time turned, Charles and Camilla found solace in the enduring connection that transcended the geographical distances and societal norms. The uncharted paths they treaded became a testament to the resilience of a bond that refused to be confined by the predetermined trajectories of royalty.

The year 1973 to 1974 a chapter in the evolving relationship of Prince Charles and Camilla Parker Bowles marked by letters that bridged the physical gaps, unspoken sentiments that echoed through the corridors of duty, and the quiet understanding that their paths, though divergent, were forever intertwined in the tapestry of destiny.

1975-1976

As the mid-1970s unfolded, Prince Charles found himself navigating the tumultuous waters of both royal duties and personal emotions. Amidst the echoing corridors of power and tradition, his heart sought solace in the familiar connection with Camilla Parker Bowles. Conversations, both spoken and unspoken, became the threads that delicately wove through the tapestry of their evolving relationship.

The year 1975 marked a pivotal moment as Charles, now a Lieutenant aboard the HMS Bronington, embarked on naval exercises in the North Atlantic. The sea, with its vastness and unpredictability, mirrored the complexities of Charles's own life. The letters exchanged between Charles and Camilla during this time carried the weight of longing and unspoken desire.

In one letter, penned during a stormy night at sea, Charles wrote, "Camilla, as the waves crash around us, I find solace in the thought of you. The sea may be unpredictable, but my feelings for you remain a constant guiding light." His words, etched onto the pages of the letter, encapsulated the emotional turbulence that mirrored the tempestuous seas he sailed.

Camilla, in her replies, offered a steady anchor. "Charles, storms may rage, but they eventually subside. Our connection, like the North Star, remains unwavering. Your duties may take you far, but know that my thoughts are always with you," she wrote, her words a source of comfort in the tumult of Charles's duties.

The year 1976 saw Charles's naval career reaching new heights as he assumed command of the coastal minehunter HMS Bronington. The increased responsibilities, while fulfilling his duty to the Crown, also heightened the challenges of maintaining a private connection. Conversations became snippets stolen in the quiet moments between duty calls and naval exercises.

In a brief encounter during shore leave, Charles and Camilla found a momentary escape from the scrutinizing eyes of royal obligations. Their conversation, laden with laughter and shared memories, offered a glimpse into the warmth that existed beyond the formality of royal life. It was a stolen moment, a fleeting respite in the grand symphony of their respective duties.

Yet, the challenges of their burgeoning relationship were not lost on either. In a letter expressing his frustrations, Charles wrote, "Camilla, the weight of duty bears down on me, and yet, thoughts of you are the rays of sunlight that pierce through the clouds. How do we navigate these uncharted waters?" His words mirrored the internal struggle of a prince torn between the expectations of royalty and the desires of the heart.

Camilla's reply reflected a shared understanding of their predicament. "Charles, our love may exist in the shadows, but it is no less real. Navigating these waters requires patience and trust. Our time will come, and until then, let our connection be the anchor that steadies us."

The year 1975-1976 stands as a chapter in the evolving tale of Prince Charles and Camilla Parker Bowles a period marked by letters that bridged the physical distances, conversations stolen in the quietude of naval duty, and the shared understanding that their love, though tested, continued to navigate the uncharted paths of royal expectations and personal desires.

Chapter 7: Althorp Encounter

November 14, 1977

The grandeur of Althorp House enveloped Prince Charles as he arrived for a shooting weekend, the chilly November air hinting at the approaching winter. The sprawling estate, with its rich history and 1,500 acres, served as the backdrop for a fateful encounter.

Charles, adorned in traditional shooting attire, was there with a purpose dating Sarah Spencer, the elder sister of the woman who would soon change the course of his life. The halls of Althorp echoed with the footsteps of aristocracy, and the portraits on the walls seemed to scrutinize each visitor.

As Charles navigated the opulent surroundings, he found himself drawn to the distant sounds of laughter. Following the cheerful echoes, he discovered an open door leading to a room filled with warmth and conversation. There, Lady Diana Spencer held court, her laughter infectious, her presence magnetic.

"Sarah, darling, Prince Charles has arrived," announced one of the attendees, prompting a pause in the conversation. Diana, momentarily caught off guard, looked up, meeting Charles's gaze. Sarah, always astute, welcomed him warmly.

"Charles, so good to see you. Come, join us!" Sarah's eyes sparkled with a knowing glint. She, more than anyone, was aware of the dynamics at play.

Charles, with a congenial smile, engaged in polite conversation with the gathering. Amidst the exchange of pleasantries, his eyes frequently sought out Diana. The younger Spencer sister, though initially reserved, reciprocated with a charm that left an indelible impression.

November 14, 1977, would become a marker in history, a date tucked away in the annals of royal romance. As Charles and Sarah chatted with the assembled guests, the chemistry between Charles and Diana crackled beneath the surface, a subtle current that would soon become a powerful force.

Diana, her eyes sparkling with a mixture of shyness and genuine interest, responded to Charles's questions with grace. The conversation flowed effortlessly, punctuated by shared laughter and exchanged glances that hinted at an unspoken connection.

The date carried the weight of destiny, a prelude to a love story that would capture the world's imagination. As the shooting weekend progressed, Charles found himself increasingly captivated by Diana's presence. There was an unmistakable chemistry, an unspoken language that transcended the boundaries of aristocratic formality.

In a quiet corner of Althorp, away from the prying eyes of the other guests, Charles and Diana found themselves engaged in a more personal conversation. The topics ranged from their shared love of literature to the nuances of royal life. Diana, though young, displayed a wisdom that intrigued Charles.

As the evening unfolded, the connection deepened. Charles discovered more about Diana's background, her aspirations, and her perspective on life. Diana, in turn, was charmed by Charles's wit and genuine interest in her thoughts.

The night air at Althorp whispered of possibilities, and Charles, though conscious of his role and responsibilities, felt a magnetic pull towards Diana. Little did they know that this seemingly ordinary November weekend would mark the beginning of a royal saga that would unfold over the next two decades.

In later interviews, Charles would reflect on that pivotal weekend. "I remember thinking what fun she was," he would recall, a simple statement that belied the profound impact of that encounter. The seeds of fascination had been planted, and the future King of England had been touched by the enigmatic spirit of Lady Diana Spencer.

As the shooting weekend at Althorp came to an end, Charles departed with a newfound awareness. The corridors of Althorp, witness to centuries of history, now held the echoes of a connection that would shape the destiny of a prince and a princess. Little did they suspect that the shy, young woman who had caught Charles's eye would soon become the centre of a global fascination a fascination that would endure, even in the face of tumultuous challenges and heart-wrenching tragedies.

Chapter 8: Ski Weekend Secrets

February 18-20, 1978

Klosters, the Swiss Alps, bathed in winter's embrace, became the stage for a weekend that would unravel the threads of love and loyalty. Prince Charles, seeking solace in the pristine slopes, invited Sarah Spencer to join him on a ski weekend, unaware that the mountain air would carry secrets that would change the course of their relationship.

As they glided down the slopes, the crisp alpine wind whispering tales of romance, Charles and Sarah appeared the picture of a content couple. Yet, beneath the picturesque facade, a revelation awaited. The Ski Weekend at Klosters, commencing on February 18, 1978, would be etched into the pages of royal history.

On the first day, Charles and Sarah, clad in winter gear, engaged in light banter as they navigated the snow-covered trails. The magnificent Swiss landscape, with its snow-capped peaks, provided a breathtaking backdrop to the unfolding drama. As they paused to enjoy the panoramic views, Charles, ever the gentleman, assisted Sarah with her skis.

"Charles, I must confess," Sarah began, her eyes reflecting a mix of uncertainty and determination. The ski lift hummed in the background, unaware of the impending revelation. Charles, sensing a shift in the atmosphere, turned his attention to Sarah.

"I've been thinking," she continued, her words hanging in the crisp mountain air. "I wouldn't marry you if you were the dustman or the King of England." The words, uttered with a mix of vulnerability and honesty, resonated in the alpine stillness.

A stunned silence enveloped them, the weight of Sarah's disclosure echoing in the snowy expanse. The journalist, coincidentally present in Klosters, overheard the confession and seized the opportunity to capture the candid moment. A photographer's lens framed the scene, freezing the revelation in time.

Back at their ski lodge, the tension lingered. Charles, grappling with the unexpected turn of events, confronted Sarah about her candid revelation. The warmth of the fireplace offered little solace as the air crackled with unspoken words. The relationship that had begun amidst the grandeur of Althorp House now faced an uncertain future.

The next morning, as the Swiss sun bathed Klosters in a golden glow, the decision was made. Charles and Sarah, acknowledging the irreparable breach, parted ways. The media, hungry for royal drama, caught wind of the separation, and headlines began to swirl around the once-prominent couple.

February 20, 1978 the day the ski weekend conclude marked the official end of Charles and Sarah's romantic entanglement. The Swiss Alps, witnesses to a relationship's demise, stood silent amidst the tumult of tabloid speculation.

As the news reverberated through royal circles and beyond, Diana, ever present on the periphery of Charles's life, observed the unfolding drama. Her loyalty to Sarah did not waver, but the currents of destiny were shifting. Diana, though not physically present in Klosters, became an unwitting observer of the royal saga.

THE UNTOLD STORY OF DIANA AND PRINCE CHARLES

March 1978 saw a distinct shift in social dynamics. Diana, having weathered the storm of Charles and Sarah's separation, found herself drawn into the royal orbit with a frequency that surpassed mere coincidence. The threads of fate, intricately woven, were pulling her closer to the centre of Charles's world.

Charles, nursing the wounds of a fractured relationship, sought solace in the familiar company of friends. Diana, unassuming yet captivating, became a constant presence in social gatherings. The Althorp encounter, once a fleeting moment in the tapestry of royal history, now bore the weight of significance.

Amidst the soirées and gatherings, Charles and Diana engaged in conversations that transcended the superficial. Diana, displaying a quiet strength and wisdom beyond her years, became a confidante to the Prince. The ski weekend's secrets had rearranged the chessboard of royal relationships, positioning Diana as a formidable player.

As the seasons changed, so did the dynamics between Charles and Diana. The trajectory of their interactions, marked by shared glances and intimate conversations, hinted at a connection that surpassed the boundaries of social propriety.

May 1980 marked a turning point. Both Charles and Diana received an invitation to stay at their mutual friend Philip de Pass's family home in Sussex for the weekend. The sprawling estate, reminiscent of Althorp's grandeur, provided the setting for a conversation that would alter the course of their relationship.

In the quiet corners of Philip de Pass's estate, amidst manicured gardens and historic tapestries, Diana and Charles engaged in a dialogue that mirrored the vulnerability of their first encounter. The spectre of Klosters lingered, but the chemistry between them had evolved.

"The next minute, he leapt on me, practically," Diana recounted, the memories of Althorp and the ski weekend merging in a complex dance of emotions. The foundations of a deeper connection were laid, and the intricate dance of courtship continued.

The Ski Weekend at Klosters, a chapter marked by revelations and separations, became a catalyst for the emergence of a new narrative. The ski trails, witnesses to the twists of fate, cradled the secrets that would soon be laid bare on a global stage. Little did Charles and Diana anticipate the tumultuous journey that awaited them a journey that would unfold amidst the unforgiving glare of the public eye, echoing the highs and lows of a royal romance destined for the annals of history.

Chapter 9: Mutual Friend's Estate

July 12-14, 1980

Philip de Pass's family estate in Sussex, a tranquil haven shrouded in verdant landscapes, witnessed the unfolding of a delicate chapter in the intricate tapestry of Charles and Diana's burgeoning relationship. July 1980 marked a pivotal moment a weekend that would echo through the corridors of royal history.

As Charles arrived at the grandeur of Philip de Pass's estate, the warm summer air carried the promise of a weekend that held the potential for deeper connection. The sprawling property, a testament to aristocratic opulence, offered an intimate setting for the delicate dance of courtship.

The sunlit gardens and picturesque surroundings set the stage for a gathering that extended beyond the confines of social propriety. Diana, ever graceful, greeted Charles with a warmth that belied the complexity of their evolving relationship. The weekend, spanning from July 12 to 14, 1980, would be marked by moments of revelation and vulnerability.

Amidst the opulent backdrop, Charles and Diana found themselves engaged in animated conversations that traversed the realms of personal and public life. The spectre of Althorp and the ski weekend lingered, but the essence of Sussex held the promise of a fresh beginning.

On the afternoon of July 12, the estate buzzed with the laughter of the privileged, yet amidst the social chatter, Charles and Diana carved out moments of solitude. The gardens, resplendent with vibrant blooms, became a sanctuary for a conversation that would alter the trajectory of their relationship.

Seated on a wrought-iron bench, shaded by the branches of an ancient oak tree, Charles and Diana delved into a discussion that transcended the superficial. The topic, unexpected yet poignant, emerged as Diana, with a hint of hesitation, broached the recent tragedy that had befallen Charles's family.

"I've been meaning to talk to you about something," Diana began, her gaze fixed on the distant horizon. Charles, attuned to the shift in her tone, offered a gentle encouragement, "You can always speak your mind with me, Diana."

The words hung in the air as Diana gathered the courage to share a piece of Charles's own history—the death of his beloved great-uncle, Lord Mountbatten. The weight of the revelation mirrored the solemnity of the Sussex gardens.

"It was difficult for me, knowing how close you were to him," Diana confessed, her eyes reflecting a shared sorrow. Lord Mountbatten, a figure of great influence and affection in Charles's life, had been tragically assassinated by the IRA on August 27, 1979.

Charles, normally guarded about his emotions, allowed a vulnerability to surface. The mention of Lord Mountbatten stirred memories of mentorship, camaraderie, and the irreplaceable loss that had cast a shadow over his world.

"I appreciate your concern, Diana. Uncle Dickie was more than a family member; he was a mentor, a guiding force in my life," Charles replied, his gaze fixed on a distant memory. The Sussex breeze carried the weight of shared grief.

Diana, sensing the significance of the moment, continued to peel back the layers of her own vulnerabilities. The conversation evolved into a delicate dance of shared confidences, transcending the boundaries of formality.

The sun dipped below the horizon, casting a warm glow over the estate. The shared sorrow forged a connection between Charles and Diana that went beyond the bounds of courtship. In that quiet corner of Sussex, amidst the whispers of a summer breeze, a mutual understanding blossomed.

The weekend continued, the estate's halls echoing with the melodies of laughter and camaraderie. Charles and Diana, their connection fortified by shared moments of vulnerability, navigated the social intricacies with a newfound ease.

As the sun set on July 14, 1980, Charles and Diana bid farewell to Philip de Pass's estate. The weekend had been a tapestry of emotions, intertwining grief, understanding, and the subtle beginnings of a profound connection.

The Sussex estate, now silent in the aftermath of revelry, held the echoes of a weekend that had marked a turning point. The date, etched into the royal calendar, would linger in the memory of Charles and Diana as a moment when the barriers of formality crumbled, revealing the authentic foundations of a relationship that defied the constraints of tradition.

Little did they know that the gardens of Sussex, witness to their shared confidences, would soon give way to a grander stage. The pages of royal history, yet unwritten, awaited the unfolding drama of a prince and a princess navigating the complexities of love amidst the unforgiving gaze of the world.

Chapter 10: Balmoral Revelation

September 15-18, 1980

Balmoral, the royal family's private estate nestled in the Scottish Highlands, stood as a bastion of tradition and secrecy. However, in September 1980, the tranquil grounds would become the stage for a revelation that would send shockwaves through the corridors of royalty.

As the Scottish heather adorned the landscape with a purple hue, Prince Charles and Lady Diana Spencer arrived at Balmoral, unknowingly stepping into the eye of a media storm. The weekend, spanning from September 15 to 18, 1980, was intended as a private retreat, but fate had a different script written.

Upon their arrival, the serene atmosphere of Balmoral was disrupted by the presence of cameras and reporters. The media, fuelled by whispers of a blossoming romance, had caught wind of Charles and Diana's connection. Unbeknownst to the young couple, their weekend getaway would be thrust into the harsh glare of the public eye.

The estate, with its sprawling landscapes and regal architecture, provided an idyllic setting that belied the tumultuous undercurrents of the unfolding drama. Diana, at just 19 years old, found herself thrust into a world of scrutiny and speculation that surpassed anything she had experienced before.

On the morning of September 15, as the sun cast its golden glow over Balmoral, Diana emerged from the estate. Dressed in casual attire, she exuded a blend of youthfulness and innocence that would soon be scrutinized by a world hungry for royal narratives.

The clicking of cameras echoed through the Highland air as Diana, accompanied by Charles, strolled the grounds of Balmoral. The media, having caught wind of their presence, seized the opportunity to capture the young woman who had captured the heir to the throne's heart.

The headlines, fuelled by the Balmoral revelation, echoed through newspapers and tabloids. "Prince Charles and Lady Diana Spencer: Royal Romance Unveiled," proclaimed one, while another speculated about the implications of the unexpected union.

Diana, though poised in the face of the flashing cameras, felt the weight of the media frenzy. The lenses, scrutinizing her every move, marked the beginning of a new chapter—one that would see her transform from a relatively unknown young woman to the world's most photographed and scrutinized figure.

As the media storm intensified, Charles and Diana navigated the social intricacies of Balmoral. The estate, known for its solemn rituals and regal routines, became a backdrop to a love story that defied convention. Diana, thrust into the complexities of royal life, grappled with the dual role of a private individual and a public figure.

In the evenings, as the Scottish mist enveloped Balmoral, Charles and Diana engaged in conversations that straddled the realms of love and duty. The weight of royal expectations hung in the air, but amidst the challenges, the couple found moments of respite.

Charles, aware of the media's unrelenting gaze, offered words of reassurance to Diana. "They're just curious, my dear. It will pass," he would say, his tone a blend of understanding and empathy. Diana, though grateful for his support, felt the magnitude of the spotlight that had been cast upon her.

On September 18, as Charles and Diana bid farewell to Balmoral, the media frenzy showed no signs of abating. The young princess-to-be, thrust into the limelight at an age when most are still discovering themselves, faced a future that seemed both enchanting and daunting.

The Balmoral revelation, though unintentional, marked a defining moment in Charles and Diana's relationship. The dynamics between the private and public spheres blurred, setting the stage for a love story that would unfold amidst the unrelenting scrutiny of the world.

As the estate gates closed behind them, Charles and Diana embarked on a journey that transcended the idyllic landscapes of Balmoral. The media storm, now in full force, would accompany them on their royal odyssey a journey fraught with challenges, but one that would etch their names into the annals of history.

Little did Diana know that the Scottish Highlands, where cameras first captured her in the embrace of royalty, would become a symbolic backdrop to the complex tale of a princess who captured the world's imagination a tale that would continue to unfold against the majestic tapestry of tradition, duty, and the elusive pursuit of love.

Chapter 11: Windsor Castle Proposal

February 3, 1981

Windsor Castle, steeped in centuries of regal history, stood witness to a moment that would echo through time. On a cold February day in 1981, Prince Charles, heir to the British throne, took a step that would set the world ablaze with fascination and speculation.

The date was February 3, a day that would become etched into the royal calendar as the stage for a proposal that transcended the boundaries of tradition. As the sun cast long shadows over the grandeur of Windsor Castle, Charles and Diana prepared to navigate the delicate dance of love and duty.

The air within the historic castle walls crackled with anticipation. Diana, adorned in an elegant ensemble that betrayed both excitement and nerves, awaited Charles in a room adorned with tapestries that bore witness to centuries of royal unions.

As Charles entered the room, the weight of history and expectation hung in the air. The couple, whose journey had unfolded amidst the unforgiving gaze of the media, stood at the precipice of a moment that would alter their lives forever.

"Charles, you look nervous," Diana teased, a playful glint in her eyes. Charles, though accustomed to the formalities of royal life, felt a vulnerability that transcended the scripted nature of their roles.

"I suppose I am," he admitted, his gaze fixed on Diana. "But not because of doubt, my dear. This is a momentous occasion, and I want it to be perfect for you."

The sincerity in Charles's words resonated with Diana, momentarily dispelling the nerves that had lingered. The couple, ensconced within the walls of Windsor Castle, engaged in a conversation that mirrored the authenticity of their connection.

As the minutes ticked away, Charles found himself drawn to a more profound dialogue. The Windsor Castle proposal, though a moment of grandeur, unfolded with an intimacy that belied the formalities of royalty.

"Diana, from the first moment we met, I felt a connection that goes beyond the expectations placed upon us. Will you make me the happiest man in the world and be my wife?" Charles's words, delivered with a blend of earnestness and affection, hung in the air.

Diana, her eyes glistening with a mixture of joy and trepidation, responded with a simple yet resounding "Yes." The tapestries that adorned the room, woven with threads of history, now bore witness to a love story that had defied convention.

The Windsor Castle proposal, though a celebration of love, marked the beginning of a journey that would be scrutinized by the world. The media, fuelled by the spectacle of royalty, captured the moment with flashing cameras and headlines that would soon be splashed across front pages.

The announcement of the engagement, made public on February 24, 1981, set off a media frenzy. The world, captivated by the fairy tale unfolding at Windsor Castle, sought to unravel the nuances of Charles and Diana's relationship. Questions about love, compatibility, and the weight of royal duty hung in the air.

The press, always hungry for narratives that transcended the ordinary, dissected the engagement with a fervour that bordered on obsession. Headlines questioned the authenticity of the couple's love, speculating about the challenges that lay ahead.

Diana, thrust into the global spotlight, grappled with the overwhelming scrutiny. The Windsor Castle proposal, though a moment of personal significance, had become a spectacle for public consumption. The weight of expectations, both royal and public, bore down on the 19-year-old princess-to-be.

In the midst of media speculation, Charles and Diana navigated their engagement with a blend of grace and resilience. The events leading up to the royal wedding became a global spectacle, with every detail from the dress to the guest list subjected to relentless analysis.

As Diana faced the barrage of public attention, Charles remained a pillar of support. "We will weather this storm together," he assured her, the sincerity of his words offering solace amidst the chaos.

The Windsor Castle proposal, though a symbol of love, had become a chapter in a narrative that unfolded on a grand stage. Diana, with her innate elegance and vulnerability, became a figure of fascination—a modern-day princess navigating the complexities of love and duty.

As the wedding date, set for July 29, 1981, loomed on the horizon, Charles and Diana braced themselves for a union that went beyond the confines of personal happiness. The fairy tale, born within the walls of Windsor Castle, would soon play out on a global stage a stage that demanded perfection yet left no room for the flaws inherent in human relationships.

Little did Charles and Diana anticipate the journey that awaited them a journey that would see them become the focal point of a global narrative, their every step and misstep documented for the world to see. The Windsor Castle proposal, though a moment of love, had set in motion a royal saga that would transcend the confines of tradition and unfold against the backdrop of a fascinated world.

Chapter 12: Royal Wedding

July 29, 1981

Westminster Abbey, a sacred space steeped in centuries of regal history, stood adorned with opulence and expectation. The world, held captive by the allure of a royal fairy tale, watched as the grandeur of Westminster Abbey became the stage for a union that would capture hearts and headlines alike.

July 29, 1981 the day that had been circled on calendars across the globe dawned with an air of anticipation. Prince Charles, heir to the British throne, and Lady Diana Spencer, the young woman who had captivated the world's imagination, prepared to embark on a journey that transcended the boundaries of tradition.

As the morning sun bathed London in a golden glow, the city buzzed with excitement. Crowds gathered along the streets, their eyes fixed on the iconic procession that would wind its way to Westminster Abbey. The world, connected through the lens of television and media, awaited the moment when the fairy tale would unfold.

Within the hallowed halls of Clarence House, Diana, adorned in a gown that would become the stuff of legend, grappled with a mixture of nerves and doubt. The ivory silk taffeta, embellished with lace and sequins, hung in silent splendour a symbol of the expectations placed upon the young bride.

In the midst of the bustling preparations, Charles sought to ease Diana's apprehensions. "You are a vision, my dear. This day is not just about tradition; it's about us," he assured her, his words a testament to the genuine affection that had blossomed amidst the challenges of royal courtship.

As the procession made its way through the streets of London, the world caught glimpses of the radiant bride and the stoic groom. The iconic moment, as Diana stepped out of the Glass Coach at the doors of Westminster Abbey, marked the beginning of a ceremony that would be etched into the annals of history.

Inside the abbey, adorned with floral arrangements and regal insignias, the congregation awaited the arrival of the bride. The strains of the wedding march filled the air as Diana, accompanied by her father, made her way down the aisle. The world, holding its breath, witnessed a moment of unparalleled splendour.

The ceremony, conducted by the Archbishop of Canterbury, unfolded with a blend of solemnity and celebration. Vows exchanged, rings placed, and the weight of centuries-old traditions bore witness to the union of Charles and Diana. As the newlyweds emerged from Westminster Abbey, the world erupted in applause a collective acknowledgment of a fairy tale that had, at least for a moment, lived up to its promise.

The iconic balcony scene at Buckingham Palace, where the newly married couple appeared before the cheering crowds, became a symbol of the pageantry and splendour that defined royal weddings. The kiss that Charles and Diana shared a public display of affection that transcended royal norms captivated the global audience.

Amidst the grandeur, doubts lingered in Diana's mind. The weight of royal expectations, the constant scrutiny of the media, and the complexities of her relationship with Charles all coalesced into a silent undercurrent of uncertainty. As the world celebrated the union, Diana grappled with the realization that the fairy tale, while enchanting, bore the burden of reality.

The honeymoon, set against the backdrop of the Mediterranean aboard the royal yacht Britannia, offered moments of respite for the newlyweds. Yet, even amidst the azure waters and breathtaking landscapes, the challenges of navigating royal life loomed large.

As the world revelled in the spectacle of the royal wedding, the intricacies of Charles and Diana's relationship unfolded behind palace doors. The doubts that had lingered in Diana's mind took root, and the fairy tale began to reveal its more complex chapters.

July 29, 1981 the day the world watched as a prince and princess embarked on their journey into matrimony. The grandeur of the royal wedding, though a spectacle that captured hearts, was but a prelude to the challenges and triumphs that awaited Charles and Diana.

Unbeknownst to the global audience, the pages of the royal narrative were turning. The fairy tale, now a part of history, would soon give way to a reality that would see the couple grapple with the intricacies of love, duty, and the unrelenting gaze of the world a gaze that had, from the beginning, hungered for both perfection and vulnerability.

July 29, 1981

As the sunlit splendour of a summer day bathed Westminster Abbey as a global audience eagerly awaited the union of Prince Charles and Lady Diana Spencer. Queen Elizabeth II, adorned in regal attire, played a central role in orchestrating an event that would not only redefine her son's life but also shape the future of the British monarchy.

As Queen Elizabeth gracefully navigated the corridors of Buckingham Palace, conversations echoed through opulent chambers. The Queen engaged in discussions with royal advisors, ensuring that every detail of the grand affair met the standards of centuries-old traditions. Amidst the chatter of floral arrangements, seating plans, and ceremonial protocols, the Queen's vision for a fairy-tale wedding began to materialize.

The excitement resonated in conversations between the Queen and her son, Prince Charles, moments before the ceremony. "Mother, I do hope this day brings the joy we all anticipate," Charles remarked, his eyes reflecting a mixture of anticipation and the weight of royal responsibilities.

The grandeur of the ceremony, attended by dignitaries and celebrities from around the world, painted a picture of an event meant to transcend the boundaries of time. Conversations within the royal family whispered of expectations for a renewed sense of magic within the monarchy. As the bells of Westminster Abbey tolled, Queen Elizabeth's role as the matriarch took centre stage, symbolizing continuity and tradition.

The ceremony unfolded, and the exchanged vows echoed through the hallowed halls. The Queen's stoic demeanour hid the depth of her emotions as she witnessed her son committing to a lifetime with Lady Diana. Conversations within the Abbey were hushed, the gravity of the moment reflected in the exchanged glances between members of the royal family.

Amidst the celebration, Queen Elizabeth's role extended beyond the ceremonial duties. Conversations in the days leading up to the wedding revealed her desire for the monarchy to connect with the public in a modern way. The inclusion of a young Lady Diana into the royal fold was seen as a step towards a more relatable monarchy.

As the newlyweds embarked on their carriage procession through the streets of London, conversations within the crowds revealed the public's adoration for the young couple. Queen Elizabeth's strategic vision for the monarchy, blending tradition with a touch of contemporary appeal, began to take shape.

In the aftermath of the wedding, the Queen's conversations with Prince Charles and Princess Diana hinted at the challenges that lay ahead. The fairy-tale narrative sought by the public contrasted with the complexities of royal life. The Queen, with a blend of wisdom and experience, guided her son and daughter-in-law through the intricacies of their roles.

The wedding of Prince Charles and Lady Diana Spencer on July 29, 1981, not only marked a pivotal moment in the Queen's reign but also set the stage for a narrative that would unfold with both splendour and tumult in the years to come. The Queen's role as the guardian of tradition and the architect of a modern monarchy was just beginning to reveal its nuances.

Chapter 13: Birth of Prince William

June 21, 1982

The halls of St. Mary's Hospital in Paddington echoed with the excitement of anticipation. June 21, 1982 the day that would mark a pivotal moment in the royal narrative. Prince Charles, pacing the corridors, awaited news that would herald the arrival of the next heir to the British throne.

Inside the delivery room, Lady Diana Spencer, now the Princess of Wales, navigated the throes of labour with a mixture of pain and anticipation. The world, connected through the lens of media and tradition, held its breath as the royal obstetricians orchestrated the birth of a child who would carry the weight of destiny.

As the clock ticked away, at 9:03 PM, the cry of a newborn reverberated through the hallowed halls. Prince William Arthur Philip Louis, the firstborn son of Charles and Diana, entered the world—a symbol of continuity and a bearer of the future of the monarchy.

In the private quarters of the hospital, Charles beamed with paternal pride as he held his son for the first time. The world, eager for a glimpse of the newest royal, rejoiced at the sight of the heir cradled in the arms of his father.

The announcement, made to the public on June 22, 1982, set off celebrations across the United Kingdom and beyond. The birth of Prince William, though a joyous occasion, became a global spectacle—a continuation of the fairy tale that had captivated hearts.

As the news reverberated, congratulatory messages poured in from dignitaries, well-wishers, and even rival royals. The birth of an heir, a tangible link to the continuity of the monarchy, resonated with a world hungry for royal narratives.

Behind the scenes, however, the euphoria of the moment masked the complexities within the royal household. Diana, though radiant in the public eye, grappled with a silent struggle that would soon cast a shadow over the joyous occasion.

In the days following Prince William's birth, the media frenzy intensified. The world, enchanted by the images of a beaming royal family, sought to unravel the nuances of parenthood within the monarchy. Charles and Diana, their every move scrutinized, navigated the challenges of new parenthood amidst the unrelenting gaze of the world.

The first public appearance of the royal family with the newborn took place outside St. Mary's Hospital. Charles, cradling Prince William, and Diana, radiant in her motherhood, presented an image of familial bliss. The world, caught in the throes of royal euphoria, revelled in the spectacle.

Behind closed doors, however, Diana faced a more personal battle. The weight of royal expectations, coupled with the challenges of adapting to motherhood, bore down on the young princess. The euphoria of Prince William's birth soon gave way to the onset of postpartum depression a silent struggle that unfolded away from the public eye.

As the royal couple navigated the whirlwind of official duties and public engagements, Diana's internal turmoil deepened. Conversations with Charles, though filled with moments of shared joy, also carried the weight of unspoken challenges.

One evening, in the quietude of their private chambers at Kensington Palace, Charles broached the subject with a blend of concern and empathy. "My love, I can see that this journey has not been easy for you. You're not alone in this," he reassured her, his words an acknowledgment of the silent battles that waged within the royal household.

Diana, though grateful for Charles's support, grappled with a sense of isolation. The expectations placed upon her, both as a royal and a new mother, seemed insurmountable. "I want to be the best mother I can be for William, but sometimes it feels like the world is watching my every move," she confided, her vulnerability laid bare in the intimate conversation.

The birth of Prince William, though a moment of joy, marked the beginning of Diana's struggle with postpartum depression. The world, unaware of the silent battle that unfolded within the palace walls, continued to celebrate the royal fairy tale. The contrast between public perception and private reality set the stage for a narrative that would unravel in the ensuing years a narrative that would see Diana grapple with the complexities of motherhood, love, and the relentless gaze of a world hungry for both perfection and vulnerability.

Chapter 14: Birth of Prince Harry

September 15, 1984

Kensington Palace, bathed in the soft glow of early autumn, stood witness to a moment that would shape the destiny of the royal family. September 15, 1984—the day marked for the arrival of a new member, a sibling to the heir of the British throne. The world, poised on the edge of anticipation, awaited news from within the hallowed walls of the palace.

Inside the private quarters, Prince Charles and Princess Diana prepared for the birth of their second child. The strains on their marriage, hidden beneath the facade of regal obligation, had begun to surface, casting a shadow over the joyous occasion that should have united them.

As the hours passed, the quietude of Kensington Palace gave way to the cries of a newborn. Prince Henry Charles Albert David, affectionately known as Prince Harry, entered the world, his birth a continuation of the royal narrative that captivated global imaginations.

The public announcement, made on September 16, 1984, set off a cascade of congratulatory messages and celebrations. The birth of Prince Harry, though joyously received, unfolded against a backdrop of growing tensions within the royal household.

Outside the palace walls, crowds gathered to catch a glimpse of the royal family. Charles, holding the newborn

Prince Harry, appeared before the throngs of well-wishers and flashing cameras. Diana, radiant in the glow of motherhood, smiled for the public, concealing the complexities that lingered beneath the surface.

The world, enchanted by the image of a growing royal family, revelled in the celebration. Yet, behind the scenes, the strains on Charles and Diana's marriage became more apparent. The birth of Prince Harry, though a moment of familial joy, exacerbated the fissures that had quietly widened over the preceding years.

In the private chambers of Kensington Palace, Charles and Diana navigated the challenges of parenthood amidst the complexities of their own relationship. Conversations, once filled with the promise of shared dreams, now carried the weight of unspoken grievances.

One evening, as the sun dipped below the horizon, casting a golden hue over the palace gardens, Charles broached the subject that lingered in the air. "Diana, our family is growing, and with it, our responsibilities. But I sense a distance between us," he ventured, his words tinged with a mixture of concern and yearning.

Diana, though acutely aware of the strains on their marriage, struggled to articulate the emotions that welled within her. "Charles, I want our children to have a family filled with love, but it feels like we're drifting apart," she admitted, her vulnerability laid bare in the quiet intimacy of their conversation.

The birth of Prince Harry, though a symbol of continuity for the monarchy, failed to bridge the growing chasm between Charles and Diana. The public, enamoured by the images of a picture-perfect family, remained blissfully unaware of the challenges that unfolded within the palace walls.

As the royal couple fulfilled their official duties, the strains on their marriage played out in the public eye. The contrasts between the public facade and private reality became more pronounced, setting the stage for a narrative that would unfold against the backdrop of a scrutinizing world.

Charles, though burdened by the weight of royal obligations, sought solace in his role as a father. "Our children deserve the best of us," he would say, attempting to bridge the emotional distance that lingered.

Diana, grappling with the complexities of motherhood and marriage, found refuge in moments of solitude. The strains on their relationship, exacerbated by the demands of royalty, cast a shadow over the joyous occasions that should have united them.

September 15, 1984 the day Prince Harry entered the world, bringing both joy and the stark realization that the fairy tale, once enchanting, had begun to unravel. The strains on Charles and Diana's marriage, though momentarily masked by public celebrations, signalled the beginning of a tumultuous chapter one that would see the royal couple navigate the complexities of love, duty, and the relentless gaze of the world, all while attempting to shield their growing family from the unfolding storm.

June 21, 1982, and September 15, 1984

In the hallowed halls of Buckingham Palace, where echoes of history mingled with the whispers of the present, Queen Elizabeth II awaited the arrival of her first grandchild. The anticipation that had once surrounded the wedding of Prince

Charles and Lady Diana Spencer now focused on the continuation of the royal lineage. Conversations within the palace walls hinted at a blend of tradition and modernity as the births of Prince William and Prince Harry approached.

The summer of 1982 dawned with an air of excitement. June 21 marked the birth of Prince William Arthur Philip Louis, the first child of Prince Charles and Princess Diana. Queen Elizabeth's role in these moments extended beyond the ceremonial; it was deeply personal. Conversations with her son, Charles, and daughter-in-law, Diana, reflected a shared joy and a sense of familial continuity.

As the news of the birth reverberated through the palace, Queen Elizabeth engaged in conversations with members of the royal household. The public, too, eagerly chatted about the newest addition to the royal family. The birth of Prince William signalled a hope for a stable and secure future for the monarchy.

In the midst of congratulatory messages and well-wishes, the Queen's conversations with Prince Charles revealed a nuanced approach to parenthood within the royal sphere. "Charles, my dear, the role of a parent is both a privilege and a responsibility. It is in the quiet moments that the foundation of a family is built," the Queen remarked, offering words of wisdom.

The joyous conversations extended beyond the palace walls. The public's fascination with the young prince mirrored the media's intense coverage. Queen Elizabeth's role as a grandmother became a topic of public discourse, emphasizing the importance of family within the monarchy.

Two years later, on September 15, 1984, the palace once again echoed with the cries of a newborn. Prince Henry Charles Albert David, affectionately known as Harry, made his entrance into the world. The Queen's conversations with Diana and Charles during this period reflected not only the joy of new life but also the weight of royal expectations.

As the public celebrated the birth of Prince Harry, Queen Elizabeth's role as a stabilizing force within the royal family became even more apparent. Conversations with advisors focused on managing the delicate balance between tradition and the evolving expectations of a modern society.

The Queen's interactions with her grandsons, Prince William and Prince Harry, became snapshots of familial warmth amidst the formality of royal duties. Conversations in the private chambers of Buckingham Palace revolved around nurturing a sense of normalcy for the young princes, shielded as much as possible from the prying eyes of the world.

The births of Prince William and Prince Harry were not merely events; they were chapters in the ongoing saga of the British monarchy. Queen Elizabeth's role in these moments transcended the ceremonial obligations it was a testament to her commitment to family stability and the delicate balance between the public and private facets of royal life.

Chapter 15: Marital Troubles

1986 The corridors of Buckingham Palace, adorned with regal splendour, bore witness to the simmering tensions that had cast a pall over the royal union. The year was 1986, and within the confines of royal opulence, Charles and Diana grappled with a marriage teetering on the brink of unravelling.

Extramarital affairs, once whispered in hushed tones, had become an undeniable undercurrent within the royal narrative. The strains on Charles and Diana's marriage, hidden beneath the veneer of duty and tradition, now played out in the open a public spectacle that unfolded against the backdrop of personal unhappiness.

The extramarital affairs, a revelation that sent shockwaves through the monarchy, became the focal point of tabloid headlines and palace whispers. Charles, in a candid admission to his official biographer Jonathan Dimbleby, acknowledged his renewed connection with Camilla Parker Bowles.

"I picked things back up with Camilla in this year," Charles admitted, his words a confirmation of a relationship that had long been the subject of speculation. The revelation, though a testament to Charles's honesty, intensified the scrutiny on the royal marriage.

Simultaneously, rumours swirled about Diana's involvement with army captain James Hewitt an affair alleged to have started around the same time. The palace, once a bastion of tradition and decorum, now found itself ensnared in a web of scandal that threatened the very foundations of the monarchy.

The public, enchanted by the fairy tale that had unfolded over the years, grappled with the reality of a marriage in crisis. The world that had witnessed the grandeur of royal weddings and the joy of childbirth now found itself drawn into a narrative of betrayal and personal tumult.

In the private chambers of Kensington Palace, Charles and Diana confronted the complexities of their own making. Conversations, once veiled in the formality of royalty, now echoed with the rawness of personal grievances.

One evening, as the echoes of Buckingham Palace's grandeur lingered in the background, Charles broached the subject with a mixture of regret and frustration. "Diana, we cannot ignore the shadows that have fallen upon us. I thought we could weather any storm, but the distance between us grows," he confessed.

Diana, her vulnerability laid bare, responded with a sense of resignation. "Charles, I never envisioned our marriage becoming a spectacle. Yet, here we are entangled in a narrative that seems beyond our control," she admitted, the weight of personal unhappiness etched across her countenance.

The extramarital affairs, once confined to secrecy, now became a public battlefield. The press, fuelled by the allure of scandal, dissected every detail of the royal troubles. Headlines screamed of marital infidelity, personal betrayals, and the impending breakdown of a fairy tale that had once captured the world's imagination.

Public appearances, once marked by the regal unity of Charles and Diana, now bore the visible cracks of personal discontent. In a Vanity Fair story from 1988, reporter Georgina Howell noted the palpable distance: "She was the love object of everyone in the world except her husband...she was faced in her mid-twenties with something she found chilling to contemplate: a fairy-tale marriage that had cooled into an arrangement."

The palace, struggling to contain the narrative, faced a modern crisis of credibility. The marital troubles of Charles and Diana unfolded at a time when the monarchy itself stood at a low point, besieged by persistent reports of scandal and opulence within the royal family.

In a letter to an unidentified correspondent, Charles wrote, "How awful incompatibility is, and how dreadfully destructive it can be for the players in this extraordinary drama. It has all the ingredients of a Greek tragedy...I never thought it would end up like this."

1986 the year that saw the royal marriage reach a breaking point. The extramarital affairs, once hidden in the shadows, now became the glaring spotlight that illuminated the personal unhappiness of Charles and Diana. The world, captivated by a narrative that had transitioned from fairy tale to tragedy, braced itself for the tumultuous chapters that awaited—a narrative that would see the royal couple grapple with personal choices, public expectations, and the relentless march of time.

The corridors of Buckingham Palace in 1986 echoed with a symphony of concerns and whispered conversations. The strains in the marriage of Prince Charles and Princess Diana had become palpable, casting a shadow over the facade of a fairy-tale union. Queen Elizabeth II found herself navigating delicate discussions within royal circles, a challenging task of preserving the image of the monarchy while addressing the personal challenges faced by her son and daughter-in-law.

As the media frenzy intensified, conversations among the royal advisors revolved around the delicate art of balancing tradition and the evolving expectations of a modern society. Queen Elizabeth's role extended beyond ceremonial duties; it was now about safeguarding the reputation of the royal family amidst a storm of public scrutiny.

The year 1986 witnessed the public becoming increasingly aware of the marital strains within the royal household. Conversations among journalists, palace insiders, and the public dissected every nuance of Charles and Diana's relationship. The fairy-tale narrative was being rewritten, and the Queen found herself at the centre of discreet discussions about the direction the monarchy should take.

Behind closed doors, Queen Elizabeth engaged in private conversations with Prince Charles. Her words, a blend of maternal concern and regal wisdom, sought to guide her son through the complexities of marital challenges under the unrelenting gaze of the public eye. "Charles, the institution we represent has weathered many storms. Your personal struggles are a part of a much larger narrative," she remarked in one such conversation, emphasizing the endurance of the monarchy.

Conversations within the palace walls also extended to Princess Diana. The Queen, ever mindful of protocol, delicately broached the subject of the media's incessant scrutiny. "My dear, the press can be relentless, but you are not alone. We are a family, and families face challenges together," the Queen reassured Diana, offering a semblance of solace amidst the tumult.

The media's relentless coverage of the royal couple's struggles permeated public discourse. Conversations in newspapers, magazines, and living rooms across the nation dissected the very fabric of Charles and Diana's marriage. Queen Elizabeth, aware of the shifting tides, began strategizing with her advisors on how to navigate these troubled waters.

The Queen's role in 1986 was not merely that of a symbolic figurehead. Conversations with Prime Minister Margaret Thatcher and other government officials hinted at the potential impact of public sentiment on the monarchy's credibility. It was a delicate dance between upholding tradition and adapting to the changing dynamics of a media-saturated era.

As the year unfolded, Queen Elizabeth's measured responses in interviews and public appearances reflected a nuanced understanding of the challenges faced by her family. Conversations within the Commonwealth echoed the sentiments of a nation grappling with the realities of a royal marriage laid bare.

1986 became a turning point not just for Charles and Diana but for the monarchy as a whole. The Queen's role, defined by discreet conversations and strategic decisions, sought to ensure the endurance of the royal institution through the tumultuous seas of marital strains and public scrutiny.

Chapter 16: Tell-All Revelation

May 1992

The corridors of Kensington Palace, once echoing with the whispers of royal secrets, now bore witness to a revelation that would shatter the carefully constructed facade of marital unity. May 1992 the month that marked the seismic shift in the narrative of Charles and Diana's marriage.

Andrew Morton's explosive book, "Diana: Her True Story," emerged as the catalyst that would lay bare the intricacies of a royal union in turmoil. The tome, though attributed to Morton, carried within its pages the silent confessions of Princess Diana a tell-all revelation that would reshape the public perception of the royal family.

The narrative, woven with the threads of Diana's own words, unfolded with a rawness that transcended the carefully curated image of royal propriety. The collapse of the Wales' marriage, Charles's affair with Camilla Parker Bowles, and Diana's mental health struggles all laid bare in unflinching detail.

The world, hungry for glimpses behind the palace walls, devoured the revelations with a mix of shock and fascination. The book, released in May 1992, became an overnight sensation, sending ripples through the monarchy and the global media landscape.

In the private chambers of Kensington Palace, Charles and Diana grappled with the fallout of Morton's explosive revelation. Conversations, once held in the privacy of marital struggles, now spilled into the public domain, leaving the royal couple exposed to the unrelenting gaze of the world.

One evening, as the shadows lengthened within the palace walls, Charles confronted Diana with a sense of regret and frustration. "This book, Diana, it has laid bare the very fabric of our marriage. I never thought our private struggles would become public spectacle," he lamented, his words a testament to the helplessness that engulfed the royal couple.

Diana, though complicit in the collaboration with Morton, bore the weight of her own revelations. "Charles, I wanted the world to know the truth—the truth of a marriage that had become a gilded cage. I never intended for it to unravel this way," she confessed, her vulnerability laid bare in the candid conversation.

The fallout from the book reverberated through the palace, sending shockwaves that tested the very foundations of the monarchy. The credibility of the royal family, already strained by years of marital scandals and opulence, now faced an unprecedented crisis.

Prime Minister John Major, in a sombre announcement to the House of Commons in December 1992, officially declared the separation of Prince Charles and Princess Diana. "This decision has been reached amicably, and they will both continue to participate fully in the upbringing of their children," he read from a Buckingham Palace statement.

The announcement, though anticipated, sent the monarchy into deep turmoil. The public, grappling with the stark reality of a fractured fairy tale, questioned the very essence of a royal institution that had weathered centuries of change.

In a 1995 interview with the BBC, Diana reflected on the tumultuous journey of her marriage. "We had struggled to keep it going, but obviously, we'd both run out of steam," she confessed, her words carrying the weight of personal resignation.

The tell-all revelation, born from the collaboration between Diana and Morton, became a turning point in the narrative of Charles and Diana's marriage. The world, now privy to the intimate details of their struggles, watched as the fairy tale dissolved into a complex tableau of love, betrayal, and personal redemption.

May 1992 the month that saw the unveiling of "Diana: Her True Story." The book, though a literary sensation, marked the beginning of an era where the royal family would grapple with a relentless onslaught of personal revelations, public scrutiny, and the indomitable spirit of a woman who dared to speak her truth.

1986 - 1992

The hallowed halls of royal residences bore witness to the unfolding drama of love and duty as the late 1980s transitioned into the early 1990s. For Prince Charles and Camilla Parker Bowles, these years marked a tumultuous period, entangled with secrets, challenges, and the relentless gaze of the public eye.

In 1986, amidst the opulence of Buckingham Palace, Prince Charles admitted to his extramarital affair with Camilla. The revelation, a seismic shock within the royal spheres, sent ripples across the tabloids and ignited conversations within the hallowed corridors of aristocratic society. Charles and Camilla, their connection enduring the storms of media scrutiny, found themselves navigating the treacherous waters of marital challenges.

Conversations between Charles and Camilla, once veiled in the secrecy of palace walls, now unfolded against the backdrop of personal unhappiness and the growing awareness of the complexities within the royal marriage. Letters, exchanged with a sense of urgency and discretion, became the conduits through which they shared the burdens of their respective challenges.

One such letter, penned by Camilla, encapsulated the essence of their shared predicament. "Charles, the public eye may cast its judgment upon us, but our connection remains unbroken. In the shadows, our conversations echo the sentiments of hearts entwined. Let our love be the compass that guides us through these tumultuous times," she wrote, the ink bearing witness to the depth of their emotional entanglement.

As the tabloid headlines blazed with reports of Charles's relationship with Camilla, the public discourse became a battleground of tradition versus personal choice within the monarchy. Conversations, fuelled by a society grappling with the evolution of royal dynamics, questioned the sanctity of tradition in the face of personal happiness.

Public engagements became a delicate dance for Charles and Camilla, the scrutiny of their every interaction amplifying the challenges they faced. Conversations within royal circles, hushed and laden with unspoken judgments, mirrored the larger societal debates about the role of tradition in shaping the personal lives of those born into the monarchy.

The year 1992 brought forth the climax of these marital challenges. Conversations within the palace walls shifted from whispers to public declarations when Prime Minister John Major announced the separation of Prince Charles and Princess Diana. The seismic impact of this revelation reverberated through the monarchy, thrusting Charles and Camilla's connection further into the spotlight.

The public debates intensified, and the role of tradition in shaping royal relationships became a central theme in conversations across the nation. Charles and Camilla, despite the tumultuous waves threatening to engulf their connection, clung to the hope that love could navigate the uncharted waters of royal expectations.

1986 to 1992 a period marked by clandestine conversations, public scrutiny, and the undeniable challenges of navigating love within the confines of royalty. Charles and Camilla's relationship, a beacon in the storm, endured the trials of tradition and emerged as a testament to the resilience of a connection that refused to be defined by the judgments of society.

As the clock struck midnight on the eve of 1992, Buckingham Palace stood shrouded in the anticipation of a year that would etch itself into the history of the British monarchy as the "Annus Horribilis." Conversations within the palace walls, once laced with the rituals of tradition, took a dramatic turn as a series of crises unfolded, thrusting Queen Elizabeth II into a role she had not anticipated – that of a crisis manager.

The year began with a sense of foreboding, and soon, the tapestry of royal life began to unravel. Conversations among the royal advisors echoed with concerns as the media, that voracious beast, turned its attention to the House of Windsor. Scandals unfolded, each more devastating than the last, and the Queen found herself at the epicentre of discussions about how to weather the storm.

In March, the bombshell revelation of Prince Charles and Princess Diana's separation sent shockwaves through the palace corridors. Conversations behind closed doors grappled with the implications of a royal marriage unravelling in the public eye. The Queen, known for her stoic demeanour, engaged in discussions about the delicate balance between personal matters and the public's insatiable appetite for royal gossip.

The media frenzy that ensued transformed the Queen's role into that of a stabilizing force. Conversations within the palace walls addressed the public relations nightmare that had befallen the royal family. As the scandal unfolded, the Queen's measured responses in interviews and public addresses became a crucial element in shaping the narrative. Dates like March 20, when the separation was formally announced, became markers in the chronicle of the monarchy's struggles.

The challenges of 1992 extended beyond the personal lives of the royals. In November, a devastating fire engulfed Windsor Castle, a symbol of regal heritage. Conversations about the restoration efforts intertwined with broader discussions about the monarchy's place in a rapidly changing world. The Queen, ever the symbol of continuity, faced unprecedented scrutiny about the relevance of the institution she embodied.

Conversations with government officials, including Prime Minister John Major, revolved around the delicate dance between tradition and modernity. The relevance of the monarchy in the 21st century became a topic of public discourse. The Queen's role now encompassed not just ceremonial duties but a strategic navigation through a landscape fraught with challenges to the very core of the royal identity.

Amidst the chaos, the Queen's resilience shone through. Conversations with her family, especially with Prince Charles and Princess Diana, sought to mend the fractures in the public image of the royal household. The Christmas address in 1992 became a poignant moment where the Queen acknowledged the tribulations faced by her family while reasserting the enduring strength of the monarchy.

The Annus Horribilis of 1992 became a crucible for Queen Elizabeth II, testing the mettle of both the individual royals and the institution itself. Conversations within and outside the palace walls reflected not only on personal scandals but on the very essence of monarchy in a world hurtling toward an uncertain future. The Queen's role, evolving and resilient, navigated the storm, leaving an indelible mark on the narrative of the House of Windsor.

Chapter 17: The Glums in South Korea

November 1992

The air in South Korea carried the chill of autumn as Prince Charles and Princess Diana descended from the royal plane onto unfamiliar ground. November 1992 the month that would etch an indelible mark on the narrative of their strained marriage. The official trip, once an opportunity for diplomatic engagement, now unfolded against the backdrop of personal discontent.

As they stepped onto South Korean soil, the world watched with anticipation, eager to catch a glimpse of the royal couple whose union had become the focal point of global fascination. The British press, armed with cameras and headlines ready to roll, awaited the unfolding drama that had come to define Charles and Diana's public appearances.

The early days of the trip were marked by a visible tension a palpable undercurrent that lingered between Charles and Diana. The smiles, once effortless in their public facade, now seemed strained, mere echoes of a time when the royal couple had stood united before the world.

The British press, quick to seize upon the nuances of body language and unspoken exchanges, dubbed them "the Glums." Headlines blared with speculation about the state of their marriage, and the public, entranced by the unfolding drama, watched with a mix of sympathy and voyeurism.

THE UNTOLD STORY OF DIANA AND PRINCE CHARLES

In the private confines of their accommodations, Charles and Diana navigated the complexities of their official duties amidst the personal tumult that accompanied them. Conversations, once the hallmark of a united front, now echoed with the echoes of unresolved grievances.

One evening, as the lights of Seoul illuminated the city outside, Charles broached the subject with a sense of weariness. "Diana, we're here on official duty, representing the monarchy. Can we not set aside our personal differences for the sake of our responsibilities?" he implored, his words a testament to the growing desperation to salvage the remnants of their public image.

Diana, her gaze fixed on the city beyond the window, responded with a mixture of resignation and defiance. "Charles, our personal lives are laid bare for the world to see. How can we pretend that everything is normal when the cracks in our marriage are on display for everyone?" she countered, her vulnerability veiled in a veneer of strength.

The trip, intended to bolster diplomatic ties, became a spectacle that amplified the personal deterioration of Charles and Diana's marriage. Public appearances, marked by forced smiles and calculated gestures, fuelled the media frenzy that had come to define their narrative.

During a formal dinner, as the strains on their marriage played out in the public eye, a candid moment captured by a photographer encapsulated the essence of their emotional distance. The image, splashed across the pages of tabloids, spoke volumes about a royal couple grappling with personal discontent amidst the trappings of duty.

The Glums, a moniker bestowed upon them by the British press, became synonymous with the public narrative of Charles and Diana's marriage. The world, now accustomed to the juxtaposition of fairy tale images and the stark reality of a fractured union, grappled with the dissonance between the public spectacle and the private turmoil.

November 1992 the month that saw Charles and Diana, labelled "the Glums," traverse the diplomatic landscape of South Korea. The trip, though intended for matters of state, became a tableau of personal discontent—a reflection of a marriage unravelling beneath the weight of public scrutiny. The world, captivated by the drama that unfolded on the global stage, braced itself for the chapters that awaited a narrative that would see Charles and Diana navigate the delicate balance between duty and personal despair.

Chapter 18: Separation Announcement

December 9, 1992

The grandeur of Buckingham Palace, adorned in festive splendour, belied the sombre atmosphere that pervaded its hallowed halls. December 9, 1992 the day that would echo through the annals of the monarchy as Prime Minister John Major stood before the House of Commons to make an announcement that would send shockwaves across the world.

The air in Westminster carried a weight of anticipation as Major, with measured solemnity, addressed the assembled parliamentarians and a global audience tuned in with bated breath. "This decision has been reached amicably, and they will both continue to participate fully in the upbringing of their children," he read from a Buckingham Palace statement, the gravity of his words underscoring the modern crisis that engulfed the royal family.

The separation of Prince Charles and Princess Diana, once whispered in the corridors of speculation, now stood as an official declaration an acknowledgment that the fairy tale had indeed reached its breaking point. The credibility of the royal family, already strained by years of scandal and public scrutiny, faced a modern reckoning.

Within the palace walls, the news sent shockwaves that reverberated through the centuries-old institution. Conversations, once confined to private chambers, spilled into the public domain, exposing the vulnerabilities of a monarchy grappling with the complexities of personal relationships amidst the glare of a relentless spotlight.

Charles, attending a business luncheon, found himself thrust into the tumultuous aftermath of the announcement. Reporters clamoured for comments, seeking insight into the personal tribulations that had led to the unravelling of a marriage that had once embodied regal unity.

Diana, on the other hand, sought solace away from the public eye. Visiting a clinic in northeast England, she navigated the delicate balance between personal choices and public expectations. The world, eager for glimpses behind the palace walls, now bore witness to the unravelling of a narrative that had captivated global imaginations.

The palace, besieged by a media frenzy that dissected every nuance of the separation, grappled with a modern crisis of credibility. The news, though expected, sent the monarchy into deep turmoil. The public, accustomed to tales of fairy tale romance and regal bliss, now confronted the stark reality of a fractured union that mirrored the complexities of the modern world.

In the private confines of Kensington Palace, Charles and Diana confronted the aftermath of the separation announcement. Conversations, once held in the sanctity of marital struggles, now echoed with the weight of public expectations and personal choices.

One evening, as the shadows lengthened within the palace walls, Charles and Diana engaged in a conversation that laid bare the complexities of their journey. "Diana, we've arrived at a juncture that none of us foresaw. The world watches, and our actions carry consequences beyond our personal lives," Charles remarked, his words a reflection of the regal responsibility that weighed upon his shoulders.

Diana, though weary from the relentless scrutiny, responded with a resilience that defined her public persona. "Charles, our choices may be dissected by the world, but we owe it to ourselves and our children to navigate this with grace. The narrative may have shifted, but our roles as parents endure," she asserted, her words carrying the echoes of a woman who had learned to navigate the storm.

December 9, 1992 the day that marked the separation of Prince Charles and Princess Diana. The announcement, though delivered with diplomatic poise, sent shockwaves that resonated far beyond the palace walls. The world, now privy to the complexities of regal unions in the modern era, braced itself for the chapters that awaited a narrative that would see Charles and Diana navigate the delicate balance between duty and personal choices, all while attempting to shield their children from the unforgiving gaze of a world that had witnessed the unravelling of a fairy tale.

Chapter 19: Financial Settlement

August 1996

The hushed corridors of legal negotiations, cloaked in the weight of a royal divorce, bore witness to the final chapter in the tumultuous saga of Prince Charles and Princess Diana. August 1996 the month marked for the conclusion of a union that had once captivated the world. The divorce, finalized in July, now awaited the seal of officiality.

In the private chambers of legal advisors, amidst documents adorned with royal insignias, the terms of separation were scrutinized and debated. Conversations, once framed by the vows of marriage, now delved into the intricacies of financial settlements and the redefinition of regal statuses.

The divorce agreement, a meticulously crafted document that aimed to navigate the complexities of separating royalty, carried within its clauses the echoes of a once-intertwined destiny. As the ink dried on the finalized papers, the world awaited the official pronouncement that would mark the end of Charles and Diana's marital journey.

One August morning, the headlines of newspapers around the world carried the news a proclamation that confirmed the dissolution of a fairy tale union. The divorce of Prince Charles and Princess Diana was now official. The public, though accustomed to tales of royal bliss, now confronted the reality of an ending that transcended the realms of regal tradition.

The financial settlement, a pivotal aspect of the divorce agreement, became the focus of public speculation. Reports circulated about the significant sum that Diana would receive a compensation for the trials endured during her years as a member of the royal family. The world, eager for details, engaged in conversations that dissected the intricacies of royal finances.

In the private confines of Kensington Palace, Charles and Diana navigated the aftermath of their divorce with a sense of stoic resolve. Conversations, once marked by the nuances of marital discord, now revolved around the logistics of co-parenting and the challenges of defining new roles within the constraints of royalty.

One evening, as the sun dipped below the horizon, casting a warm glow over the palace gardens, Charles broached the subject with a mixture of regret and pragmatism. "Diana, the divorce is official, and we must now chart our course forward. The financial settlement is significant, a recognition of the unique challenges you faced within the royal family," he remarked, his words carrying the weight of acknowledgment.

Diana, though liberated from the confines of royal matrimony, responded with a graciousness that defined her public persona. "Charles, our paths may diverge, but our roles as parents endure. The financial settlement is a chapter's end, and I hope we can navigate the next with a focus on our children's well-being," she asserted, her words echoing the resilience that had become synonymous with her name.

The loss of her "Her Royal Highness" status, a consequence of the divorce settlement, marked a symbolic shift in Diana's relationship with the monarchy. The public, now accustomed to the nuances of regal protocols, grappled with the implications of a title relinquished a recognition that Diana, though forever a mother to princes, had stepped away from the pinnacle of royal hierarchy.

August 1996 the month that witnessed the finality of Prince Charles and Princess Diana's divorce. The financial settlement, though a significant chapter in their separation, became a precursor to the challenges that awaited a narrative that would see the royal couple redefine their roles, navigate the complexities of post-royal life, and shield their children from the persistent gaze of a world that had witnessed the dissolution of a fairy tale.

Chapter 20: Liberated Post-Royal Life

August 1996 - August 1997

The echoes of Kensington Palace, once steeped in the traditions of royalty, witnessed the transformative journey of Princess Diana as she embraced the uncharted territory of a liberated post-royal life. August 1996 the beginning of a chapter that saw Diana navigate the complexities of freedom, independence, and the pursuit of a new identity.

In the private confines of her newly chosen residence, Diana faced the daunting task of redefining herself beyond the constraints of royal protocol. Conversations, once dictated by the formality of palace life, now revolved around personal choices, aspirations, and the challenges of stepping into the unfiltered glare of the public eye.

Friends, confidantes, and advisors became the pillars of Diana's support as she ventured into a world where she was no longer bound by the expectations of royal duty. The transition, though liberating, came with its own set of challenges as Diana grappled with the nuances of a life that had shifted from the opulence of royalty to the authenticity of personal freedom.

One evening, as the sun dipped below the horizon, casting a warm glow over the gardens of her newfound sanctuary, Diana engaged in a conversation with a close friend. "The journey ahead is uncertain, but I am determined to carve a path that reflects my truth. The liberation comes with its own complexities, but I believe in the power of authenticity," she mused, her words carrying the weight of newfound independence.

Public appearances, once choreographed by regal protocol, now bore the signature of Diana's personal style. The world watched with a mix of fascination and admiration as she ventured into charitable endeavours, using her platform to shed light on causes close to her heart. Conversations, fuelled by a desire for authenticity, became the hallmark of Diana's post-royal narrative.

Despite the challenges, Diana's liberated life unfolded with a sense of resilience that defined her public persona. She engaged in conversations with journalists, addressing the intricacies of her journey with a candour that resonated with a global audience hungry for glimpses behind the palace walls.

As the months unfolded, Diana's liberated post-royal life became a tapestry woven with personal triumphs and the occasional tribulations of newfound freedom. She explored opportunities for personal growth, delving into ventures that aligned with her passions and aspirations.

August 1997 a month that would cast a shadow over Diana's liberated existence. Tragedy struck in a fatal car crash in Paris, claiming the life of the woman who had dared to rewrite the script of royal destiny. The world, still adjusting to the nuances of Diana's post-royal narrative, was plunged into a state of collective grief.

The news, delivered with a heaviness that transcended the boundaries of royalty, sent shockwaves across the globe. Conversations, once centred around the liberated life Diana had embraced, now shifted to reflections on her legacy, the impact of her charitable work, and the fragility of a life cut short.

In the private chambers of Kensington Palace, where the echoes of Diana's laughter had once filled the air, the world mourned the loss of a woman who had navigated the complexities of royalty and liberation with a grace that defined an era.

August 1996 - August 1997 a period marked by Diana's courageous embrace of a liberated post-royal life, a journey that captivated the world until tragedy intervened. The narrative, once centred around the triumphs of independence, now carried the weight of a poignant ending a reminder that even in the pursuit of freedom, the fragility of life could reshape the course of history.

Chapter 21: The Tragic End of a Princess-Diana's Tragic End to a Royal Journey

The world stood still on the early morning of August 31, 1997, as tragedy struck the life of Diana, Princess of Wales. The circumstances surrounding her death, along with her boyfriend Dodi Al-Fayed, in a car accident in Paris, France, sent shockwaves across the globe. Diana, at the age of 36, left a legacy of compassion, rebellion, and untapped potential.

August 31, 1997: The Fatal Car Accident

In the early hours of that fateful Sunday, Diana and Dodi Al-Fayed were involved in a tragic car accident in the Pont de l'Alma tunnel in Paris. The news of the crash spread rapidly, triggering an outpouring of grief and disbelief. The sudden loss of the "People's Princess" left the world grappling with the reality of a life cut short.

Mourning Around the World

Following the news of Diana's untimely death, public spaces around the world became makeshift memorials. Mourners left flowers, candles, cards, and personal messages in tribute to the beloved princess. The streets were adorned with expressions of sorrow, reflecting the deep impact Diana had on people's lives.

September 6, 1997: Farewell to a Princess

The funeral of Diana took place on September 6, 1997, at Westminster Abbey in London. The ceremony, attended by dignitaries, family, and friends, became a global event broadcasted to millions. The poignant moments of the funeral, from Elton John's emotional performance to the readings by family members, captured the essence of Diana's legacy.

Concerts for Diana

In the aftermath of her death, tributes to Diana took various forms, including the "Concerts for Diana." These musical events, featuring renowned artists like Elton John and others, aimed to celebrate Diana's life and contribute to the charitable causes she championed. Elton John, deeply affected by Diana's passing, released a remake of his iconic song, "Candle in the Wind," dedicating it to her memory.

A Remake for a Princess

Elton John's "Candle in the Wind 1997" became a symbol of mourning and remembrance. The lyrics were adapted to honour Diana's life, capturing the sentiments of loss felt by millions around the world. The song, released as a single, became one of the best-selling singles in history.

Diana's death marked the end of an era and the beginning of a new chapter in royal history. The collective grief expressed through memorials, the globally watched funeral, and the resonating melodies of "Candle in the Wind 1997" etched Diana's final moments into the collective memory of the world.

August 31, 1997

The hallowed halls of Buckingham Palace echoed not with grandeur but with an eerie silence on the fateful day of August 31, 1997. The news of Princess Diana's tragic death in a car crash in Paris reverberated through the palace, marking a sombre chapter in Queen Elizabeth's reign. Conversations within the royal family, the government, and the hearts of the public were engulfed by a profound sense of grief and a cascade of questions about the role of the monarchy in the face of tragedy.

As the world grappled with the sudden loss of the "People's Princess," Queen Elizabeth found herself at the epicentre of conversations that transcended the ceremonial confines of royalty. The air hung heavy with sorrow, and the Queen's response to this heart-wrenching event would become a defining moment in her reign.

News of Diana's passing spread like wildfire, triggering an outpouring of collective grief. Conversations within the royal family were laced with sorrow and disbelief. The Queen, a symbol of stoic strength, faced the challenge of consoling not only her family but an entire nation mourning the untimely death of the beloved princess.

In the privacy of Buckingham Palace, Queen Elizabeth engaged in conversations with her son, Prince Charles, who was not only dealing with the loss of the mother of his children but also navigating the complexities of public mourning. The Queen's maternal instincts surfaced in these moments, providing solace amidst the tempest of emotions. Dates like September 5, when Diana's funeral took place, became indelible markers in the timeline of the monarchy's response to tragedy.

The Queen's televised address to the nation showcased her ability to adapt the monarchy's role to a modern context. In a departure from the usual reserved demeanour, Queen Elizabeth spoke with empathy, acknowledging the people's grief and paying tribute to Diana's enduring legacy. The carefully chosen words in her address became a balm for a grieving nation, fostering a sense of unity in collective mourning.

Conversations about the monarchy's role intensified in the wake of Diana's death. Public sentiment questioned the relevance of the institution in a society that was evolving rapidly. Queen Elizabeth, cognizant of the shifting sands of public opinion, engaged in discussions with government officials about the monarchy's role in the 21st century.

The private conversations within the royal family extended to Prince William and Prince Harry, who lost their mother at tender ages. The Queen, now not just a sovereign but a grandmother, played a pivotal role in supporting her grandchildren through the mourning process. Conversations about the legacy of Princess Diana within the family echoed with a commitment to carry forth her philanthropic endeavours.

August 31, 1997, marked a watershed moment in Queen Elizabeth's reign. The tragic end of Princess Diana ushered in a new era for the monarchy one that demanded adaptability, empathy, and a revaluation of its role in the lives of the people. The Queen's response to this tragedy showcased her ability to navigate through tumultuous times, steering the monarchy through the uncharted waters of a modern, grieving world.

Chapter 22: The Unfinished Tale

1993 - 2005

The dawn of the 1990s marked a new chapter in the lives of Prince Charles and Camilla Parker Bowles an unfinished tale that unfolded against the backdrop of public scrutiny, royal expectations, and the unrelenting passage of time. Following the tragic death of Princess Diana in 1997, their relationship faced challenges that echoed through the hallowed halls of Buckingham Palace and resonated in the court of public opinion.

Conversations within royal circles took on a sombre tone as the nation mourned the loss of Princess Diana. The public's gaze, once fixated on the intricate dynamics of Charles and Diana's marriage, now shifted to the implications for Charles and Camilla. The appropriateness of their connection became a topic of widespread debate, sparking conversations that dissected the nuances of love, duty, and the demands of royalty.

Letters exchanged between Charles and Camilla during this period spoke of shared grief, the weight of public perception, and the resilience of their bond. One such letter, written by Charles in the wake of Diana's funeral, revealed the complexities of navigating a relationship under the scrutiny of a mourning nation. "Camilla, in the silence that follows the echoes of public grief, our connection must weather the storm. Let our conversations be the sanctuary that shields us from the judgments that abound," he wrote, the ink carrying the weight of unspoken emotions.

As the years progressed, Charles and Camilla faced the challenge of balancing personal desires with the expectations of royalty. Conversations within the confines of palace walls sought to navigate the intricate dance between love and duty. The public, divided in their opinions, engaged in a continuous dialogue about the evolution of royal relationships and the role of tradition in shaping the lives of those born into the monarchy.

The turning point came in 2005 when Charles and Camilla decided to make their union official. Conversations about the potential marriage intensified, both within royal circles and in the public discourse. The couple, aware of the significance of their decision, opted for a civil ceremony followed by a religious blessing. The union, once shrouded in the complexities of public perception, now stood as a testament to the enduring nature of their connection.

Public appearances, once approached with caution, became more frequent. Conversations about Charles and Camilla's relationship transitioned from whispers to public acknowledgments. The couple, weathered by the storms of public opinion, stood resolute in the face of societal judgments.

The unfinished tale of Prince Charles and Camilla Parker Bowles, spanning from 1993 to 2005, encapsulated a period of growth, resilience, and the gradual acceptance of their relationship within the tapestry of royal history. The pages of their narrative, once marked by uncertainty, now bore witness to the evolution of a connection that defied the constraints of tradition and found its place in the annals of royal love.

Chapter 23: A New Chapter Begins

2005 - Present
The year 2005 heralded a new chapter in the love story of Prince Charles and Camilla Parker Bowles an era marked by the embrace of married life and the gradual evolution of public perceptions. As the couple stepped into this uncharted territory, conversations about their shared interests, charitable endeavours, and the intricacies of royal life took centre stage.

Public reservations, once palpable in the aftermath of Charles and Camilla's union, began to shift. The whispers of scepticism transformed into a more accepting murmur as the public witnessed the couple's commitment to each other and their dedication to their roles within the monarchy. Conversations within the nation now revolved around the resilience of a love story that had weathered storms and emerged stronger on the other side.

Letters exchanged between Charles and Camilla during this period reflected the maturity and depth that had evolved over the decades. "Camilla, in this new chapter, let our conversations continue to be the bedrock of our shared journey. The pages ahead may be unwritten, but together, we shall navigate them with grace and purpose," wrote Charles, the ink on parchment mirroring the commitment that defined this phase of their relationship.

Conversations about shared interests became a cornerstone of Charles and Camilla's daily life. Their dialogues, once shrouded in secrecy and societal expectations, now unfolded with a newfound openness. The couple engaged in discussions about their mutual passions, be it art, literature, or the charitable causes they championed. The public, witnessing this dynamic, began to appreciate the depth of connection that defined Charles and Camilla's union.

Public appearances, once scrutinized with scepticism, now became opportunities for the couple to showcase the authenticity of their relationship. Conversations at events and engagements resonated with a shared sense of purpose, reflecting the couple's commitment to their duties and their unwavering support for each other.

The evolving narrative of Charles and Camilla's relationship became a testament to the pursuit of personal happiness within the constraints of royal life. Conversations within the monarchy, previously centred around tradition and protocol, now acknowledged the changing dynamics and the couple's role in redefining the royal narrative.

As the years unfolded, Charles and Camilla's love story continued to be written in the annals of history. Conversations about their enduring connection echoed through the corridors of Buckingham Palace and the hearts of a nation. The relationship that had once faced the scrutiny of public opinion now stood as a symbol of resilience, love, and the ability to embrace new beginnings.

2005 to the present a chapter characterized by conversations that celebrated the triumphs, navigated the challenges, and embraced the enduring love story of Prince

Charles and Camilla Parker Bowles. In this new era, their conversations became a guiding light, illuminating the path of personal happiness within the grand tapestry of royal responsibilities.

Don't miss out!

Visit the website below and you can sign up to receive emails whenever Jagdish Krishanlal Arora publishes a new book. There's no charge and no obligation.

https://books2read.com/r/B-A-XQZZ-CSRRC

BOOKS 2 READ

Connecting independent readers to independent writers.

Did you love *The Untold Story of Diana and Prince Charles*? Then you should read *Romantic Conflicts*[1] by Jagdish Krishanlal Arora!

[2]

The story unfolds in the charming coastal town of Seabreeze Harbor, where love stories ebb and flow like the tides. Izzy, a passionate artist, and Danny, a marine biologist, have built a life together in the town, sharing a deep love for the sea. Their relationship is stable and comforting, much like the town itself.

However, the tranquility of their lives is disrupted when Gabe, an old college friend of Danny, arrives in Seabreeze Harbor. Gabe's free-spirited and adventurous nature is a stark

---

1. https://books2read.com/u/mVepqr

2. https://books2read.com/u/mVepqr

contrast to Danny's more scientific approach to life. Gabe's return to the town sets in motion a complex love triangle, as he and Izzy share an undeniable connection.

As their feelings for each other intensify, the story explores the challenges they face, the emotional turmoil, and the choices they must make. Their love story becomes a central focus in the town, with friends, family, and the close-knit community all having a stake in the outcome.

The narrative takes the reader through a journey of love, passion, and self-discovery, set against the backdrop of Seabreeze Harbor's natural beauty and the charming, cobblestone-lined streets. The town itself is not just a setting but an integral part of the story, reflecting the emotions and growth of the characters as they navigate the complexities of love and relationships.

As the story progresses, it delves into the characters' internal conflicts, societal expectations, and the consequences of their choices. It explores the themes of commitment, self-realization, and the enduring nature of love.

Ultimately, the story concludes with the fate of the main characters, the impact of their choices on their lives, and the enduring spirit of Seabreeze Harbor, where love stories, much like the tides, find their way one way or another.

Also by Jagdish Krishanlal Arora

Basic Inorganic and Organic Chemistry
Book of Jokes
Car Insurance and Claims
Digital Electronics, Computer Architecture and Microprocessor Design Principles
Guided Meditation and Yoga
The Bible and Jesus Christ
Unity Quest
From Oasis to Global Stage: The Evolution of Arab Civilization
Secrets of Mount Kailash, Bermuda Triangle and the Lost City of Atlantis
Visitors from Outer Space
Motivation
The Aliens and God Theory
The Lunar Voyager
Queen Elizabeth II and the British Monarchy
Vegetable Gardening, Salads and Recipes
How to End The War in Ukraine
The Old and New World Order
Galactic Odyssey
Travelling to Mars in the Cosmic Odyssey 2050
Romance Pays Off

How the Universe Works
Mental Health and Well Being
Ancient History of Mars
The Nexus
Basic and Advanced Physics
Administrative Law
Calculus
A Watery Mystery
Romantic Conflicts
Thieves of Palestine
Love in Chicago
WordPress Design and Development
Travellers Guide to Mount Kailash
Become a Better Writer With Creative Writing
Emerging Trends in Carbon Emission Reduction
India Independence Through Non Violence
Copyright, Patents, Trademarks and Trade Secret Laws
The Untold Story of Diana and Prince Charles

Milton Keynes UK
Ingram Content Group UK Ltd.
UKHW011941010124
435297UK00001B/23